# Blood Calls to Blood:
## The Story of Wyrd John
By
## Chris Dahl

# Blood Calls to Blood
# The Story of Wyrd John
ISBN 978-1-9079-6311-7

Published by
# Hedge Witchery Books
www.hedge-witcherybooks.com

*I warn you, you may not want to know the details of my life swimming around your head.*
*I know I wish I didn't.*

*John*

*When Light breaks through the shrouding mists*
*Awakening the Life within the Soul,*
*The Fires cascade all around you,*
*Making the Immortal whole.*
*Striving for that final Truth.*
*Beckoning It with your call,*
*Seeking out your own true self,*
*Voices ring off Hallowed Halls*
*But once you find that Ecstasy*
*Beyond the Bounds you flow,*
*Flying ever-higher into the Sunlight...*
*But Remember The Paths Below.*

## Born Under a Bad Sign: John's Birth

*"Number is the within of all things."*
Pythagoras

*In the Tale of the Ordeals and the Decision on Cuchulain's Sword, Cormac gains a cup that Mananan promised him. The bearer tells Cormac 'Let three words of falsehood be spoken under it, and it will break into three: Then let three true declarations be under it, and it unites again as it was before.*
An Ancient Irish Tale

10/16/1966 was a Sunday, the seventh day of the week and the Christian Sabbath, an ironic day, to say the least for John, the Pagan, to have been born. That Sabbath fell on a New Moon as well, a time when the moon is almost directly between the sun and the earth. Not quite an eclipse, the light is blocked and there is no reflection from the Sun to light the Moon; it is dangerous for mortals on earth to catch a glimpse of the Moon in this phase. The Baptists and Catholics of John's family would have woken early on this New Moon Sabbath and worshiped at churches, perhaps built by his ancestors, with hidden occult symbols carved into the friezes over the lintels or at cathedrals adorned with gargoyles and Green Man faces. John's mother, a self-proclaimed Hedge Witch with lineage dating back to the Old Times, would have worshiped this phase of the Moon as one that is propitious for cleansing ... or destruction. She would have taken the magic cords that held back her living room curtains and she would have cleared the wooden "coffee table" and raised it high so that it became an altar. She would have taken out her silver Quaich, drinking bowl, and begun a ceremony there in her modest home in honor of the Moon.

Instead of observing the Sabbath and worshiping this powerful New Moon, the mother was sweating in labor, bent heavy with the weight of her son, sweating and trickling blood. Finally, she gave birth to John on a 3 day:

$$10/16/1966$$
$$1+0+1+6+1+9+6+6=30$$
$$3+0=3$$
$$3$$

3, that "sacred number", as John later called it, was crucial in his life, from his birth to the day of his incarceration. This number is sacred in virtually

3

every culture and way of thinking. For the Christians and Catholics in John's brood, it would have been invoked as the basis of the Holy Trinity, the third member who is the unseen force behind things or the Holy Ghost. Mathematicians, such as the ancient Greeks, saw the 3 as associated with the strongest geometric structure known to man, the triangle, while clairvoyants such as Ann-Catherine Emmerick saw this Christian Holy Spirit as the Eye of God at the center of the mathematician's triangle. Mayans believed in the fertile properties of the number 3, associating it with women; the Chinese believed it was the perfect number. Egyptians believed that this number represented the "three elements" of the sky, the earth and the duat, or intermediary zones between the earth and spirits from the air. The Li-ji believed in another trilogy: man as the intermediary between earth and sky. In general, this sacred number, no matter what the culture – pagan, heretical or monotheistic – is perceived as a tri-point link between the physical being, the spirit and the ethereal forces in between. It is also creative.

And there was John, crying as he pushed through the blood and afterbirth and the din of his mother's moaning. He was covered in a caul, which was powerful magic. In the doctor's arms his skin was still blue as the oxygen teemed through his veins and animated him as the doctor snipped the umbilical cord, separating him and his mother, placing him in her arms. His mother looked down at him and knew what he was; she knew the power of the New Moon – it could be powerfully good or powerfully destructive. She knew the power of the number 3 and the vibrations of the Sabbath. John's mother did not believe that people were born clean and pure with white, spotless souls and empty minds just waiting to be filled. No, she knew that "blood called to blood," that certain souls ended up in certain women to be born at very specific times in history. Souls were not, as they had tried to teach her in Sunday school, spotless sheets of paper waiting to be marked upon by the smudge marks of sin; she knew they were oily rags that had absorbed eons of history after living through one age after another, one century after the next.

She looked at her son and she knew he was marked by a potential to create and, just as there is darkness for each ray of light, the potential to destroy. Though the Bible was just one book of many books for this mother and her family, she knew well enough that the bible asks if a "clean thing can come from an unclean thing." She thought of that as she looked down at the child that had just come from her womb, as her body throbbed and ached still. She didn't know the answer. She only knew that he could be a great leader, a fabulous writer or thinker – or a madman killer. Wherever he fell in the fold of things, the mother knew she would have to let John go into the big world eventually, where there were people who wouldn't understand what he was, when he had been born or the moon that hung in the sky that night. They would judge him based on some stone-age commandments or in some arbitrary court of law. They wouldn't understand that he had been taught the Truth and that he lived to tell the truth and to live true to himself and what he was born to be – whatever that may turn out to be.

And so it was in that tenth month of the year, which the pagans in the old days called the Win-monath or wine-month when they brewed elderberry wine and fermented Brown October Ale, that John came onto this plane of existence. To consecrate the day in a way that came to his mother from the Old Days when her people wandered the heaths and moors of Angle-land, the Land of Angels, she performed a ceremony on her new-born son: "She used a needle to prick my heels, palms and forehead to represent the five points of the pentagram. Around my right wrist she placed a chain of gold to represent the Sun; on my left a chain of silver for the Moon. Over my heart she placed a bit of Iron to give a strong heart and will. Water was wiped across my brow to give me fluidity of thought; honey on my tongue to sweeten my words; and a circle of willow on my genitals so that I may know the love of a woman. In my right hand she placed a hammer so that I might be skillful and in my left a blade to aid me in the art of war. 'This is my son,' she spoke, 'protect and guide him so he may know his destiny.'" Thus John was bound to the "Old Ones" before he could even walk.

He was also bound by another oracle on that bloody Sunday in that month of wine-making: three geasas were laid upon John's life. Often it is a woman who places these oracles on a child, someone who knows the Craft; they are strong and cannot be broken, lest the hero who labors under their spell become undone. John joined a long list of adventurers and heroes, one in which even the mighty Irish hero Cuchalain lived with a geasa on his soul (he was warned never to eat the meat of a dog, but he was also never to refuse food offered him by a woman. One day an old hag offered him a meal of dog meat and he was trapped and this led to his death). The same damning irony would rule John's days.

John lived with the secret of his geasas from that day forward: "Do you understand what a geasa is? It is a prohibition placed on a person, usually at birth or at the time they come of age. But also can be placed at any time by the right person. I have three geasas laid upon me:
1. Shed not the blood of a holy person nor on consecrated ground by violence.
2. If asked thrice, so long as it harm none, grant it but only once.
3. That it is a duty to stand twixt the weak and harm, shed blood and weep tears, but never waiver in this – to fail in abiding by this geasa is bad, it brings ill-luck, bad tides, misfortune to the person."

5

Like any prophecy, any oracle, geasas are borne out over time and rarely does the hero even know how, when or why the importance of that stricture will be revealed. It was not until many years later, after many miles had been covered, and after many hardships were endured, that John would see the true meaning of his inception.

# Blood Calls to Blood: John's Youth

*"Three things cannot be long hidden: the sun, the moon, and the truth".* Buddha

John's mother was a mix of European Celtic and Native American. In her lineage were two of the most powerful earth-based spiritual traditions on earth. Scotland and Ireland and certainly the Native Americans of the entire American continent – North and South – have been cradles for what the "mainstream" Christian powers have officially, down to their dictionaries, defined as "pagan" or more specifically "an adherent of a polytheistic religion in antiquity, especially when viewed in contrast to an adherent of a monotheistic religion... one who has no religion... an adherent of a religion other than Judaism, Christianity, or Islam... a hedonist," little of which resembles the actual definition of the term. Yet, some Christian fanatics go on to define the religion virtually irrelevant: "in the broadest sense includes all religions other than the true one revealed by God, and, in a narrower sense, all except Christianity, Judaism, and Mohammedanism."

"Pagan" is a term that has always polarized groups, physically, socially and mentally. During the time of the Roman Empire, the term pagan was applied to "country dwellers," as opposed to those who were metropolitan or town dwellers, which was considered more civilized and appropriate for humans. Those who lived in the crags, in the woods and in the valleys of Europe and what later became Scotland, Ireland and England were looked upon with suspicion, since they lit "bone-fires" or "bonfires" on the tops of hills when the veils between the physical and spiritual worlds were thin enough to reach through; they celebrated the movements of the sun and the moon; they mixed potions of herbs and leaves and burned them in cauldrons to influence everything from winning favor from the Gods and Goddesses of Fertility to healing an illness; they worshipped alone or together, naked or clothed, inside or outdoors – "whatever worked," to quote John's mother.

These seemingly inchoate beliefs and customs were viewed negatively most likely because they were unique and hard to control and even more difficult to define. Therefore, there was a fear that evolved around these people who followed ancient systems of belief and lived simply and in tune with the rhythms of the earth and what it produced. The metropolitan power-brokers, first of which were the Roman Emperors and later the Catholic Church needed to control and eventually exterminate this Pagan "threat". Laws were passed and the threat of death and violence was real.

The Romans started by removing the symbols of the illicit religion. First the Altar of Victory was removed from the Roman Senate. The altar was a golden idol of a Goddess named Victory, the outcome of every battle that every Roman worshiped She fluttered down from above on wings of gold, bearing a palm frond in one hand and offering a laurel wreath to the victor with the other. Next went the abolition of the Vestal Virgins, a group of priestesses who tended to a hearth that kept a perpetual fire burning, the very Soul of the Roman Republic if you will. These women took vows of chastity and purity in order to tend this flame. The emperors extinguished that fire. Laws and taxes were then levied, such as the emperors appropriating all the income of Pagan priests.

Before Christianity became the official religion of the Roman Empire, the Twelve Tables of Roman Law outlawed certain incantations and spells intended to damage cereal crops. Women were killed in 331 BC as witches in connection with an epidemic. Thus, the wily forces of nature, the ones with which the Pagans were immersed, was used as justifications to use Pagans as scapegoats. The term "witch" became an even more powerful epithet and was used for centuries in connection with Pagan persecution to justify violence and even death.

The Christians, led by the Popes, continued in an even more systematic manner. For instance, Pope Gregory "appropriated" the caverns, grottoes and valleys that were once used as sacred spots in Pagandom for celebrations. "Let altars be built and relics be placed there," said the Pope. Thus, the Pagan religion was deemed a religio illicita. With actions such as these, and many others, Pagans were forced deeper and deeper into hiding, though not necessarily out of view, even after the Catholic Church officially adopted a doctrine of religious tolerance in the 1960's. As John relates later on, his family was chased from Europe by persecution and eventually landed in America; as America became more and populated, his family of Pagans and Witches moved further and further into the wilds of the new country. Eventually, John's family, like so many other Pagan families, "hid in plain sight," imbedding symbols of their way of life: pentagrams on the cutting board. Magic cords holding back the curtains and coffee tables that converted into altars. So, the Pagan traditions, the Old Ways, as John calls them, survived, still live on and in some senses still thrive; but the animus remains between the two parties. The "apology" Pope John Paul II prayed for on March 12, 2000, was called pathetic by John: "Christians have often denied the Gospel; yielding to a mentality of power, they have violated the rights of ethnic groups and peoples, and shown contempt for their cultures and religious traditions" Thus, the Pope called for Christians to extend a laurel leaf of peace to Pagans and others. Unfortunately, the Christians destroyed the laurel leaf when they destroyed the Altar of Victory.

The history of the Pagan, complete with its attendant hatred, controversy and violence is reflected in John's own words:

*"You should make a record of your life and the craft," it was said to me on several occasions. I have hemmed and hawed over this for years, procrastinating really, unsure if this story should be. I've read the popular books about them and what I was brought up in, while having some similarities, diverges from the so-called White Witchcraft touted by the masses of Pagandom. What has occurred to me is this:*

1. *a record should be made*
2. *that record should be honest and straightforward*
3. *the record must incorporate the depths and breadths of the craft regardless of the popular view, referred to today as political correctness, for that without such a record the tradition will die out and so it will no longer exists*

*For this reason, I have put pen to paper to write this book, if only to preserve that tradition within these pages, for future generations. Now many people approach witchcraft as a religion. I think now that this is not the case. There is the religion, sure, though witchcraft is a science. While the two can and do mingle, the religion can be practiced without the craft and the craft and the practice without the religion. However, I practiced both and witchcraft. There are some people who were purists in witchcraft, only taking from a unique half or tradition. As my mother told me, "Whatever works." she was not hampered by cultural boundaries. Witchcraft is witchcraft, regardless of where it comes from. The only difference is how it is practiced, so I was given a broad range of traditions and cultures to make use of. "Whatever works." On the subject of religion, it matters not one iota at which altar you bow -- or no altar at all. When it comes to witchcraft, though, if by chance you have dedicated yourself to a god who prohibits its use, you may wish to break with that god before hand. Let's face it people, some gods are a bit petty and we've had no problem punishing a wayward follower. So break faith before reading further lest that prohibition breaks you. Beyond that, unless you seek the help of the divine being, and there are many to choose from, you should leave that god or goddess for the craft.*

*This work will not contain the totality of my life, only those key events within my experiences that will inform you. I do this not just to retain some level of personal privacy, but to keep from boring you half to death. Experiences that I do report to you will at times seem beyond believable to some of you, but I remind you all that experiences are a very personal thing, the nature of which are difficult and at times impossible to fully share with another person merely through words. At such times we obtain and the ability to share our experiences directly through a lot of words, which will have to do. With all that said, I will warn the casual reader and the uncommitted dabbler: do not take lightly what this book reveals for it will ultimately be to your own downfall. Only a fool plays with fire recklessly ....*

*I was born to a house divided. On one side my father was a military man with German blood running through his veins. I was born and bred by my mother, a self-proclaimed Hedge Witch, Welsh-Irish-Dutch and filled out with a bit of Cherokee and Blackfoot thrown in for good measure. I, the youngest and only male child of this union, my father held great hope for me and had great expectations that I would be his mirror image cast in a younger frame –such is the foolishness of parents.*

*My mother told me we came from a long line of witches much later and while I had learned this already from my sister, my mother went into greater detail about how far back this went. The first Morgans to arrive in this country came in the later part of the 1600's to escape the constraints of Welsh living. Some of my family made it as far as Ireland but some crossed the Atlantic only to find some constraints here in towns villages and cities. So they went into went into what was then the sparsely populated areas of West Virginia and the Carolinas. They set up trading posts and small communities. But as time went on more people came and once again my family had to hide their beliefs and assume a more proper public religion as they had in England.*

*These ancestors however ever feeling the chafe of this social yoke placed upon them went about hiding occult symbols in the nooks and crannies of their lives. One such ancestor who lived in Morgantown built a church and discreetly placed these symbols in plain sight for those with eyes to see.*

*But allow me to back up here, for a moment. For those who have never delved into witchcraft or similar occult science. I should point out that your first spell marks you forever. Long before my mother sat me down to explain my family to me – which by the way had more Catholics at this time and Baptists than I care to contemplate, reducing the number of witches down to 15 – myself, mom, grandma, one sister (the eldest having become an evangelical Baptist, then agnostic, back to a free-willed Christian, etc.) and a cousin among those. With a family tree as large as mine this was about half a percent. Whatever the cause, our numbers were on a down-slide.*

*As she filled me in on my family history she took me around the house revealing to me the tools of the craft. I found it interesting that everything for the most part was hidden in plain sight. The bell made of brass and silver plated stood in the china cabinet with a silver blade, both engraved with much design work. Yet it wasn't until I was shown these things that I saw in these swirling lines the Names and Symbols that mark it for what it truly was. Yet to the casual eye it would have been merely a bell or a large wedding cake knife.*

*The pentacle was a real shock to me for I had used it on many occasions to chop vegetables and the like while helping my mother in the kitchen. On the cutting surface it looked like any other chopping board. Measuring roughly one-and-a-half feet square and a few inches thick. Yet once turned over there it was, the five pointed star within a circle, done in a dark wood all inlaid and flush with the surface.*

*When I commented on it seeming sacrilegious she smiled and told me that was silly. It was a tool; one side held one purpose and the reverse held another. "If the lights went out would you refuse to the candles of an altar and stumble around in the dark?" I had to admit, she had a point.*

*The cords for magic ended up holding back the curtains in the living room. This now makes sense as you would have to close the drapes anyway. The altar was the coffee table. This having been purchased while we lived in Germany. Broad, long and dark it could be raised and lowered on a spring-loaded scissor jack type mechanism, a very useful function to be sure. The broom, of course, was something I always thought of as decorative and used sometimes as part of the Halloween decorations we sometimes put up for fun.*

*The wand was an old walking stick which was spiraled in shape and I found out later was called a shillelagh and technically a club. It looked quite old and dark from many years of use. This had no marking on it I could see but it felt... strong and ancient, with it in my hands I felt powerful. As if I could do anything. As a child I had been drawn to it as it sat leaning in the corner behind the front door, like some keep a baseball bat there. I know my great-grandfather had used it as a cane in his later years and according to my mother he was a very gifted witch in his own right.*

*Then came the one piece I had never seen before. My mother brought it out of the top of the hall closet and my eyes lit up with amazement. It was a sword in a black leather scabbard. Thin bladed like a rapier but with a cross guard instead of the usual basket. It seemed to vibrate in my hand as if I had just struck it on a stone. I was told it was a military sword from the mid-1800's and had belonged to one of my ancestors. It wasn't a ceremonial sword but one designed to be used in battle.*

*Finally, she brought out one item that served only one purpose. Stored in a velvet bag, wrapped in white silk cloth she showed me a silver bowl. It was perhaps eight inches across and three deep with two small handles on each side. This was a quaich, a drinking bowl. Some well most, witches and pagans tend to use the chalice of some type but my mother told me that this was more appropriate for "we Celtic witches." I looked at her and said, "I thought all witches had a cauldron?" Smirking like she had a tendency to do, she said, "We had one but we usually only made stew with it. Sure enough we did have one. Not a small pot but a large cast iron cauldron we could easily stand in (though only up to our knees).*

*Having been shown all these things, she told me that these things would go to me upon her death. Sadly, this wasn't to be. For my mother passed without a Will and my grandfather, who wasn't inclined to the Old Ways, took possession of it all. By the time of his passing, only one sister, the eldest and Christian, got it all. While I have done what I can to contact her, she has yet to respond to me. Such is the way of things; they pass on and are forgotten.*

*All that history, the power of objects that old, is passed from one generation to the next. In this there is power and should be preserved. Yet I know most have come to the craft on their own with no connection to their past. But as I have shown you can take items from your family and re-purpose them. If you lack this you can hunt the flea markets or antique shops, even the odd yard and estate sale. True, the items won't have that connection to your past family members, but they will contain the imprints of those who have owned them over the years. As such they can be used to tap into to assist your workings.*

*Now, after hearing about my history and being shown these things I came upon a book I am sure most of you know, A Witches Bible: The Complete Witches Handbook by Janet and Stewart Farrar. In the appendix A of part two that is entitled The Search for Old Dorothy by Doreen Valiente I was introduced to perhaps the only independent source that a Morgan was practicing witchcraft. As it clearly states… "Gerald Gardner was initiated into witchcraft in 1939 by Old Dorothy Clutterbuck, a witch of the New Forest." In her search for Dorothy Clutterbuck, Doreen traced down not only Old Dorothy but her parents as well. Thomas St. Quintin Clutterbuck, Captain of the 14th Sikhs and Ellen Anne Clutterbuck. Further research yielded Ellen's maiden name… Morgan. This was the inkling of a longer and older connection to the Craft from outside the family. Not that I don't believe but it's always good to have some things confirmed. I have had some inquiries made to try to get an in-depth genealogy done to try to confirm some familiar connection to Ellen Anne Morgan but as yet unsuccessful. Perhaps in the future, I will be able to find out more information. If there is a connection, however remote, it would not only confirm everything I have been told but would also be really cool.*

*According to my mother and grandmother blood is important. It is that which conveys life and energy but connects us to the gods and the power of all things. In our family tradition, we kept items of our ancestors as objects of power. Often times these items were small locks of hair and or lockets or boxes of dried blood. Long time ago, upon the death of a person, these things were taken form the body. In ancient times it wasn't just from family but from vanquished enemies. While some of you may not like it, heads often were taken and preserved, usually put on display. I'm not trying to resurrect that tradition, but think the hair and blood might be brought back.*

*Who am I? My name you shall not have, for I value my privacy above all else; yet if you can string together the pearls, the fortunate and committed few may have it one day. I was born in the year of the horse on a Sunday on the 289th day of the year. My first memories were of a German countryside, where my two sisters and I played in meadows or on snow-covered hills. Born with a caul like my younger sister and the gift of speech and sight, as was as my mother, I was marked for what I am, a witch with the gifts of sight, sound, touch and speech. For the caul, according to my mother, covered my entire head and my hand was caught up in its trailing edges. When I began to exhibit my powers, my father disparaged it, scoffed at it until these gifts, this very part of me, became desuetude within me for a time – at least.*

*Time went on and a part of me withered within my soul. I was too young to understand why my father disliked what I could do. I thought it would please him, for all little boys want desperately to please their fathers; but this was a part of me he did not care for and I ignored it. It laid asleep in me and weakened around him.*

*But just as my father disliked that part of me, my mother enjoyed that part of me. My younger Sister Kathleen, born with a caul as well and five years older, and who had already learned to keep certain things hidden from my father, schooled me in this. She was not only my sister, but closest friend and ally. My other Sister Jeanne was about as sensitive as a stump of wood. She was, at best, a gifted mundane. Even so, she is my sister and for better or worse, that won't change. So while my father was always negative towards my gifts, my mother tried to nurture Kathleen and myself. But my mind kept coming back to my father's reaction and so I faltered.*

*Time passed and I physically grew. We left Germany behind and my father retired from the military and there were arguments between my parents… heated, vicious fights. My sister ushered me away out of the house, but I was young and mostly I was alone. Kindergarten was not part of the school program and with Jason and Kathleen six and five years older and my mother drinking now to escape the unhappiness of her marriage, I was allowed to play and be by myself. I will not go into details – yet – but let's just say for a boy of five left without supervision the world can be a cruel place. Even in a middle class neighbor hood. And I was, like all children, adventurous and fearless. This would lead to both wonders and dangers.*

*In the town, well city, there was a park and across the street from it was an elementary school. This park was the closest bit of nature around within walking distance for me. I would go there with my sisters when my parents would argue. I suppose it was here that I had my first experience with what some call the "supernatural".*

*In this park there was this bridge over a drainage canal. Nothing huge, mind you, but it was a deep canal. Once, while at the park, I wandered away and decided to walk the railing of the bridge, just to test my balance. Below was a clutter of items washed down during a heavy rain, everything from wire fencing to shopping carts. Well, sure enough, half way or so, I slipped and over I went, falling to certain injury if not death. And yet, as unlikely as it would seem I fell into the only place where there was no debris. Wet, muddy to be sure, but whole and uninjured.*

*However, I was stuck down in this drainage canal, the sides too high and steep for me, all of 5 and a half feet, to climb out of. Though it didn't stop me from trying. Yet, try as I might, I kept sliding back down. It wasn't long before I was frustrated and scared and crying. And yet I can remember being angry that I couldn't get out. I could not begin to tell you how many times I tried to get up the side of the canal, but I do know on my last attempt something grabbed me by my shirt collar and hoisted me right up like I weighed nothing, setting me on solid ground.*

*I turned only to find a very tall man in front of me, taller than anyone I had ever seen. He was wearing no shoes, blue jeans and a grey sweatshirt even though it was summer. His hair was blond, long, falling past his shoulders. He smiled at me; well more of an amused smirk that made his eyes seem sort of friendly. I didn't notice it then but it only struck me years later that his eyes were the color of winter holly and he had pupils like a cat. His features were sharp angles and his face a long oval. To this day, I remember his words exactly…*

*"There ya go," as he set me down. Can't have you getting hurt until it's necessary." I then looked back to where I had fallen and landed, a foot either way and... well at best it would have been a trip to the hospital. When I looked back up the man was gone. I don't mean walking away... I mean GONE. It's a park, wide open spaces and you couldn't help but see him walking away. I couldn't see him anywhere. Not soon after, my sisters found me and took me home.*

*Of course, some may say that the memory is colored by my concepts later in life. Possible. I am merely relating what happened as I recall it. Yet the words are as they are.*

*Summer blossomed and school let out, though this was not of any real meaning for me being young and not having to go to kindergarten. But my sisters were 5 and 6 years older than me and didn't want their little brother tagging along. My summer started out with the back door neighbor calling me over the fence into his yard. There, he showed me a book he had of men and women engaging in sex. Being lonely, my mother starting to drink more and more to escape her unhappy marriage, my father working more to avoid my mother, my sisters spending more time with friends their own age or older, I was pretty much left alone.*

*I thought Wayne was cool. He showed me that book which no one had ever shown me. But the second time he called me over was when I first learned of the evil which lies within the minds of some people. He took me into the garage where he had a black and white kitten which he handed me, allowing me to pet it and play with it. Then he snatched it away and wrung its neck, then put it in a plastic bag, then that went into another, after which he stomped on it until it was a black, white and gray smear in the plastic. He said that if I said anything that he would hurt me, my sisters, and my family. Scared, sick to my stomach and in shock, I didn't resist. He made me climb up into the rafters on which he had a platform and a mattress on it. Wayne pulled down my shorts and underwear and raped me. When I wouldn't be quiet he stuffed a rag in my mouth.*

*Scared, hurt, confused, he let me go home where I spent the rest of the week hiding inside the house. I couldn't say anything because I truly believed the threats he made. This was only reinforced when my parents found a dead black cat on the back porch. Perhaps then and there I should have said something but I was scared. Unfortunately the fear evident on my face was read as guilt and so I was "asked," more like accused, of killing the cat. I denied it, honestly, but they didn't believe me. And so it began, the slow estrangement from my parents.*

*The rest of my summer was filled with loneliness, fear, horror and abuse and a slow death of my childhood. My mother drank more. My father worked more. My sisters avoided being home more and more as my mother became less and less friendly and more miserable, making everyone miserable around her. It all fell apart. For me, Wayne called me over two or three times a week and I was too afraid not to obey.*

*Once he had a girl there. I had never seen her before. He made us do things while he took pictures with his Instamatic camera. Then he had me take pictures of him and the girl. She was a little older than me but she was just as scared. After that one day I never saw her again and I always assumed that she ended up like the cat, which scared me even more.*

*That summer was a constant nightmare, my world gone crazy and dark. I learned through popular television re-runs of Star Trek's alien star how I might survive. If I didn't have emotions, I couldn't be hurt. Nothing would really matter. So I went within, hiding in myself. I became numb to everything, even when Wayne called me over one day only to find several older boys there in the garage. They had beer and wine and liquor and pot. They made me drink and smoke and after that each one took their turn with me. Some more than once. This was towards the end of summer and after that day Wayne never called me back over again.*

*I thought I was free of it, of the horror, the abuse. Sadly that was not to be. When school started I had to be bussed from one side of the town to the other even though there was a school not ten blocks away. This was part of the desegregation of public school program. I was to walk to this one school only to catch a bus to a school several miles away. Between my home and where I caught the bus lived the boys, older teens who had been at Wayne's house that day. However, I had protection on my walks to and from there, walking with my sisters... but this was to end.*

*Not long after school started my parents split. The scene in my front yard was horrible as my parents tore me and Kathleen from each other's arms. My sisters were to live with my father and I was to stay with my mother. Now I had no protection to and from the bus. Mornings were sneaking to the bus, avoiding the teens in between. The afternoons were the same but in reverse. Running from hiding place to hiding place, it was as if I were a downed pilot behind enemy lines, except, once captured I would face torture, humiliation and then be released to start all over again. Weekends were my safe times, where I could stay home, yet fearful I would see Wayne across the fence.*

*Months later though an eternity seems to have passed, a surprise! My beloved sister visits. She knows what my life has been like and knows the cause of my fear or at least the start of it. She, her life given over to anger, Kathleen goes across the street and brings back Joy, the preacher's youngest child. She is only six months older than me but I can see in her eyes that we share that same secret, that same fear. But Kathleen has a book, not my mother's book. She keeps that hidden, locked away in a box. No. Kathleen bought this book, on the cover is a white cat, a candle and a string of pearls (at least this is what I remember of it). She sets first about making the fear turn to anger; then pushed us to rage. Silent rage, intense hatred directed toward a single person. The person who I know hurt all three of us... Wayne.*

*We are three: that sacred number. Kathleen, Joy, myself in the backyard where I once played feeling safe but no more. I cast my first spell.*

*For those who have not done this, a caution to you: If you choose to practice witch craft let your first spell be as neutral as possible, let it be balanced in its intent, neither good nor baneful, for the first act of spell craft marks you. It will be seared into your mind and burned into your soul. It will color everything you do in witchcraft, weaken the potential of all your intent that runs counter to that first spell. If I had but known this. Kathleen, having already been casting spells was not to be marked by this spell... not so for Joy and me.*

*In the grill used to barbeque, we lit coals. I went and fetched items I had taken that belonged to the target of our hatred. Other things needed Kathleen had brought with her. She held out a sheet of paper to Joy and then to me, keeping one for herself. She cast a circle around us, speaking the words of calling, invoking the Elements and opening the gates*

*My almost forgotten talents awoke. The hairs of my head seemed to stand on end; cold power sent chills over my skin. It was a warm and sunny afternoon. Power moved around us, and I could see it like heat rising off the asphalt in the distance, distorting the view of what was beyond.*
*'Hecate! Hecate! Hecate!*
*Hear me. Assist me. Avenge me.*
*For the wrongs done*
*To my mind*
*To my spirit*
*To my body*
*Joy and I repeated the words each in turn.*
*With anger rage and fury*
*We call upon the Sisters Three*

17

*The bane of Evil*
*The Scourge of the Vile*
*The blight of the Deeds Dark'*

*Again we repeated the words.*

*Kathleen threw a handful of what I now know as herbs, dried and ground up, into the flames. They were burned and released its harsh smell and she began to read her complaints from the note in her hand. She called upon Tisiphone, speaking the charges against Wayne with an ever increasing edge to her voice. Then Kathleen nudged Joy who cast her own handful of herbs to burn calling up on Megaera, faltering a moment before speaking out her own list of grievances. Kathleen looked to me but I was caught up in my own world, my senses now alert and sharp. I'd seen the power playing about us, caressing my skin as the words spoken echoed in my mind, but never diminishing. Joy then nudged me out of my stupor. I realized Kathleen had given me a handful of herbs. The herbs were all clumped together with my sweat. I threw them into the fire, some of it sticking to my hand. I spoke the name Alecto and shivered as if doused with cold water and spoke of my own treatment to Alecto, about all of my abuse; but Wayne was but one name of a list of names and it wasn't until much later that dad and Kathleen realized the torment I'd been subjected to by Wayne and other male teens in the area. I poured all the rage into those words and the rage I felt in school until I was strangely empty, and then we burned the paper with the three names on it with the words, 'So Mote It Be!'*

*Maybe three or four weeks later, my mother and I moved away and I was never to live in that area again. What became of those people, I do not know. I never saw them again. My mother, who was utterly ignorant of what happened in the backyard that day, took me to some cousins in Richmond, Virginia. We stayed there and having my newly re-found self again did what comes natural for a child witch. But Uncle Bobby was a confirmed Born Again Evangelical Baptist or so he said when he found me in the dirt drawing "Devil" signs. He took a switch off the cherry tree and beat me with it. I couldn't even begin to tell you now what I had been drawing. Aunt Robin cleaned up the welts from the switch on my legs, and when my mother came back from work she was mad. I thought she was mad at me, so once again I made sure that my skills went back to sleep. However, it was Uncle Bobby she was mad at, but as is often the case, she passed it all off to her kids.*

*Soon after, we went to Norfolk to look after my great aunt -- not blood family, just the wife of my great uncle A.D. Morgan who was a wealthy man, now passed on by the time we arrived. It was a granite stone house, the kind of house you think of for haunting, and such as I loved it, it was as if I had come home. My great aunt didn't like noisy children, maybe because she had none herself, at least this is the impression I got. Most adults dismiss children in many ways, but most high on that list is they think children lack the ability to observe and reason things out for themselves. Children are not oblivious to what is: they may not get all the nuances but they get what is going on.*

*We arrived in July, so school was out. My mother, having been trained as a nurse, took care of my great aunt, and being a boy I explored my new surroundings: musty attics filled with mysterious treasures and a library off the formal living room where I found medical textbooks with transparencies of layered anatomy of the human body. I was fascinated by National Geographic magazines dating back to the 1920s that showed me a world beyond the boundaries of my home, where people lived, loved, faced troubles, lost and sometimes died. Animals I never knew existed were made real to me. Ancient tribal people of far-off lands, dancing around the fire, wearing masks -- the caption on one called one of them and a witch-doctor. Well I knew what a Witch was and what a doctor was. Put together, I reasoned it was a witch who healed people. Later that day, I asked my mother what a witch-doctor was. Her definition was not what I had expected, or not exactly what I had thought. But being the boy I was, my attention was soon onto something else. Without a guide, someone to keep the focus, I found another distraction.*

*The house backed up to the sound and I would go down to the seawall. It was here I found jelly fish floating in the water; their ghostly transparent bodies fascinated me. I followed them along their course and came among a wide expansive lawn with geese. I had never seen them up close and they were huge compared to me who was all of seven. I met the man who lived there (we will call him George though that isn't his name.) He let me feed the geese, play with his dogs; he paid attention to me and answered any question I could think of, not in the usual condescending way most adults seemed to do when they didn't simply dismiss my presence As much as was possible, he treated me kindly and as an equal. An adult doing this was beyond strange and I felt valued. I would go over there nearly every day except when it rained. We would have snacks on the patio overlooking the sound. Then one day he invited me upstairs after a swim in the sound for cookies and ice cream. He gave me a towel to dry off and put my clothes in the washer machine. One thing led to another and we ended up upstairs in his bedroom. George never hurt me or forced me like Wayne had. He was kind and gentle and he was nice to me. I never said a word.*

*When my mother got sick and placed in a hospital with jaundice, I was sent to my grandparents to stay. The novelty of this wore off in about a week, as*

19

*having been left to my own devices for so long I was now expected to follow rules, which I felt completely unfair. Don't do that, don't do this -- and I was expected to obey without any explanation or reason. Needless to say, I ended up in trouble most of the time.*

*My mother was released from the hospital just after school began after Thanksgiving. My great-grandmother was still alive as was my great aunt Jenny. Virginia was her real name. They were old beyond belief and, as was the custom, taken care of by the family in the home. I do not understand people today, shipping off their elders to nursing homes. It wasn't that we couldn't afford it; to be sure, we could have. But to do so would have been shameful. I learned some things from them both. My great grandmother, whom we called Big Mama, was blind but could see more than most in spite of it. Aunt Jenny was fun, though she never much cared for my kitten, Little Joe, named for the Michael Landon character in Bonanza. She would flick her fingernails on the wicker rocking chair she sat in which would drive Little Joe nuts, causing him to jump at the sound to which Aunt Jenny would shout "scat", which he would, right under the couch. Big Mama would comment that he was a mouser and Aunt Jenny would say "if he lives that long." Of course she said it with a grin and didn't mean a word of it. But Big mama and Aunt Jenny would look at me with this look as if they were not looking at me but into me. Big mama would often call me by another name, sometimes speaking in Welsh or Gaelic in a few words. Grandma would hush them when they would 'tisk at me. I never found out what they were saying, but it would make everyone uneasy at times. I did learn that they sometimes called me by a name of someone who died in the war. That would be World War Two, though exactly who it was I do not recall.*

*Mom finally found work and moved out to a one-bedroom apartment in a small beach-side town. After years of marriage and doing all that was proper by society's standards, the new-found freedom in a tourist town on the beach went to my mother's head. Yet, being a single mother I was often taken with her as she enjoyed parties. A new experience, surrounded by those adults who paid attention to me. These friends of hers would speak of Sabbats and Esbats, Gods and Goddesses, ghosts, potions and all manner of things. And people here respected my mother and my grandmother. They treated me special as well. Though, I didn't understand exactly why.*

*When I was eight, my mother moved in with Bill. There was a party most every night. People drank, smoked and danced long into the night; but, unlike before, I was sent to bed where I would lie awake listening to them. After a week of this, I became used to it. Now, I didn't like Bill from the moment I met him. There are people in this world I've met and I had instinctively disliked, and I've learned to listen to my instincts -- though a bit late. I believe had my innate abilities not been suppressed before I would have not so easily fallen into the hands of Wayne, but what has happened has happened and cannot be undone. I've often wondered what my life would have been like had I been born to parents who accepted me as I am, gifted in areas that they would allow to flourish. But I may as well ponder what the world would be like if the sun rose in the West and set in the East.*

*I refer to him as Bill the Bastard, and with good cause. Abusive when drunk and mean the rest of the time, it didn't take but two weeks before he started in. After a party when every one had left, he came into my room, waking me up by pulling off my underwear. He told me my mother had sent him in because she didn't want to do it. That he and she both agreed I wasn't worth more than shit and that I was to learn to earn my keep. His hand around my throat kept me from making noise louder than a muted squeak. He was on disability, though I couldn't tell how he was disabled, so he was home most of the time. I'd come home from school and there he was. One day he actually made me dress up as a girl. He would hurt me while he raped me, squeezing, punching, and grinding his fist into my stomach. And he did much worse. When he was too drunk to perform, he used the handle of a screwdriver. All the while he was telling me my mother said this was all I was good for. That if I didn't act like I was supposed to, they would kick me out. It would be years before I realized that it was all lies. But when you are eight and you know your mother is right there in the house, it's easy to believe what is said. I didn't find out that she had been drunk and passed out until I was an adult.*

*Bill the Bastard caused me the most harm because he not only raped me physically, hurting me only for the sake of causing pain, but he tore my psyche apart. He enjoyed making me dress up like a girl, making me act like a girl, play with girl toys while he watched before raping me. He once or twice held a knife to my genitals, threatening to cut them off and make me a girl for real. I cried, begging him not to do it, promising him anything if he wouldn't. And he made me do just that, anything he could think of. Say anything, be anything.*

*This went on for five months, living in a state of numb shock and horror. Traumatized in mind, body and spirit, I began to lash out at the world. I no longer cared for anyone and saw myself as alone. I was in trouble and all before long and soon found myself in front of a judge where I had to write a 10,000 word essay on youth in the law, much of it I copied from a book that was supposed to teach me of my bad behavior. By this time my great-grandmother and Great Aunt Jenny had passed through the Veil. My mother moved into Big Mama's bedroom and I into Aunt Jenny's room. My actions were not rational, driven by a warped*

21

*sense of the world my life had been. Anger, misplaced as it was, rendered what people said as meaningless. And so I continued to get into trouble. Before long, I was back before the judge and given a choice: Reform school or the Boy's Home. I chose the latter.*

*Boys Home was a place for troubled youths aged nine to eighteen. I was all of ten years old when I arrived there. I remember the day perfectly. It was Friday afternoon; the boys in the cottage I was to be placed were all packed up ready for a weekend camping trip. I didn't go. I was offered but I declined. By this time I was a loner; it seemed safer that way. At least no one could betray me. I spent the first three days alone in the cottage that housed 18 kids total. The cottage was one of six, each one housing boys according to age groups. Each cottage named for a different social club.*

*After the return of the boys from the camping trip I was welcomed by them, most just as damaged as myself, if slightly older, with a blanket party in the middle of the night. They covered me with a blanket, held me down and proceeded to beat me, kicking and punching me, only to finish with each one taking a turn at me. Then they scattered and said that if I said anything I'd get more of the same. I crawled out of bed, taking each step even though I was in pain, making my way to the bathroom to empty my bowels of the collective semen of perhaps 15 males. I used toilet paper to make a pad to catch the blood -- tears from inside. I never said a word. Over the next month, I came to understand there was a hierarchy in this place. It was based on who could beat up whom. The weaker and smaller ones tended to be on the bottom quite literally. It was here I learned the rules of life, the strong and good fighters ruled; the weak got trampled.*

*I started working out on the weight machines at the gym. They fed us well, even taught us boxing. However, I had learned some martial arts, Tae Kwon Do to be exact. Something I had picked up at the YMCA while living with my mother. Against an adult I was simply over-matched, against others closer to my age I was adequate. Once I started to build up strength, though never big or muscle-bound, I learned I was a lot stronger than most my size. It was perhaps four or five months after the blanket party that I beat up one of the bigger guys, Jackie, who was like four years older than me. That won me respect, but even better, it made me feared by the other boys in the cottage as he was older than the others and from another cottage. So it was that I was finally left alone. I even chased one boy, Kent, with a fire-poker. Luckily for both of us I never caught him as I had all intentions of bashing his skull.*

*Around the ninth month of my being at the Boy's Home my father suddenly shows up with my two sisters. The reunion was bittersweet as they left* me there but with promises that my father was working on coming to get me. Three months later they came again with the same promises. I waited and waited until I could not wait any longer. I ran away but was caught and returned. It was soon after this that my time at Boy's home ended. I was sent to Foster care.

So there I was, 12 years old, living in a foster home with a good woman though she was clueless how to deal with me; her answer was "church and god". Yeah, I was forced to go to church at the boys home, too, so I resented that. Word to the wise, never force feed a child religion. Being that I resented it already, I had found a strategy to deal with it, being in this case Sunday school. I went about asking questions I knew would force them to remove me from those classes, like in the case of the ark, considering the number of animals on the planet that could not survive the flood versus the available room in the cubic feet of the ark -- not to take into account the room for food and water, which didn't even enter my mind at the time. There was no way two of every animal could sit. Or if Adam and Eve were the only people plus children and if Cane slew Abel and went to Nod and found a wife, where did she come from? Unless he married his sister, which is a sin, not to mention that all the children would only have their brothers and sisters to marry. Well it only took about a month before I was asked not to come back.

I stayed at the foster home for a little while and still my father didn't show up. I ran away once to my grandparents', but was returned. The next time I ran away, I decided I'm going to my sister Jean's place who would know where my father lived, as going to my mother's or my grandparents' place just would end up having me returned to foster care. So one night I did just that. It took me the better part of 24 hours to travel about 160 miles at the age of 13, and I finally made it. I was looking forward to the warm reception I knew awaited me. Sure enough, I got to Jean's place and they contacted my father who showed up a few hours later. But as we were walking down the back steps, his first words to me in private were, "You really fucked things up this time." All the disapproval I had seen in his eyes during my early childhood, the empty promises he had given as I suffered in the boy's home, and now this at that moment. He ceased being my father in my heart, though it wasn't a flip of a switch but a slow-growing trend that ate out any love I had for the man. I owed him nothing. In fact, I owed nothing to anyone. My life had been a series of torments and in that empty space the idea started to blossom that now I was safe to be happy here [with my father] only to have that notion torn out by the roots. And now this combination from my own kin, my father, I was alone. I would always be alone and I can only rely myself for myself. Betrayed from all points, I felt. No one wanted me, cast adrift, flotsam of no value. Darkness descended and with it what tiny spark of light within me was all but snuffed out. My life had been a series of torments *interspersed with lulls in which the idea started to blossom that now I was safe and could be happy only to have that notion torn out by the roots. And now this from my own father, my kin? I was alone. I would always be alone and could only rely on myself for myself.*

*As I said, a person's first spell marks them forever. Kathleen and I had called upon the Three Furies. Alecto I called on and I felt her embrace and redress, twice marked and worse, the Furies are not so kind to males. Kathleen had misjudged, thinking of the target's gender and of my own touched by rage and being a creature of violence and retribution. I know now that I let them claim me that day and alter my past and fill me with a capacity for great violence and a sense of justice when I see a wrong not righted -- for nothing gets my blood boiling more than that.*

*There I was with the man that I once loved now slowly turning to hatred, at worst, and ambivalence at best. A few days later, could have been a few weeks, Kathleen moves back in there; her being under the same roof made him bearable.*

*While I had learned some craft at my mother's side, wither from her or one of her friends – a very loosely formed coven of mostly solitary witches coming together mainly to socialize, it was Kathleen who was more directly informative in my early years. She taught me directly while I learned from my mother by osmosis. I recall Kathleen teaching me Ogham and runes and how not just to write them, but to use them in incantation and spells. In fact she gave me my first set of runes in the first Winter Solstice we shared together under our father's roof. She took me out in the woods and said I should climb up the tree to the first limb. Once there, she told me to hang upside down by my legs. Dangling there, the blood rushing to my head, she held up each rune tab, a store-bought set with a small bag and book, naming each one as she dropped it into the bag. She told me the tale of how Odin had hung from the Great Tree, Yggdrasil, to gain wisdom. How he sacrificed his eye, half his sight of the mortal world to gain greater sight beyond. How he had descended into the Underworld and returned with the Runes. When she had finished, she told me to get down, handing me the bag. She told me to take three out one at a time. To this day I recall the three I picked:*

*First was Eihwaz and she drew the symbol into the dirt.*

*The second was Algiz and she drew that over the first.*

↑

*Third was Teiwaz and that went over the rest.*

"*This is your bind rune,*" *she said to me.* "*By this you are bound from until your death.*" *I looked down and saw the symbol etched in the dirt. I still use it to this day.*

*Eihwaz is Yggdrasil, the Tree of Creation. It bridges the realms of the mortal and the Gods. The Three Worlds reside on it. Eihwaz can be seen as a hunter, a rune of action, striving, persistence and endurance. In a magical sense it is the force which tests the Seeker and is the first rune representing the first step on a spiritual path.*

*Algiz is the symbol of protection; it also represents the energies of the Gods directed down toward Man. It is wholly spiritual in nature.*

*Teiwaz is associated with the God Tyr, who was a God who sacrificed his hand to chain Fenris the Wolf. He is also the God of Battle and war in the North. But unlike most gods of war, his is not about conquest or blood lust. Tyr fights for justice. He is the God of Justice and Bravery.*

*Interesting how the plucking of three mass-produced tiles purchased from a book store in a mall can so easily bind and entwine one's life so completely. The implication of each rune separately is nothing; when they are merged, they create meaning. I will say no more. Those with eyes to see and the desire to seek the truth may find it, or a part of it here.*

*Besides giving me my first set of runes and teaching me the Ogham, both in script and in their use in spell casting and divination, she helped me open and begin to develop my abilities. At first in was in small ways, like taking me out into the deep woods and placing me in a clearing blindfolded, forcing my other sense to compensate. Then putting ear plugs in, then clamping my nose closed, and finally wrapping me in a wet blanket. This forced me to rely on all my remaining senses, losing them one by one until none were left that I could rely fully on. Telling me to reach out with my inner senses to discern what was around me. Or, sitting in front of a candle looking into the flame seeking to control it. Or sometimes looking beyond the flame to see what it reveals.*

*She introduced me to the elements of earth, air, fire and water. She showed me the sky and the Sun and the Moon and the stars and all the animals and trees and plants. She helped me cast my perceptions about, reaching out into the world and the field of Life Energy that surrounded me. Once felt to the touch, draw it in me, let it flow through me, spin about me, shape it, give it my intent and to release it. Physical contact with the earth was important. She said that going to ritual naked is not needed but being barefoot is, to remove things like watches, glasses, being freshly bathed without foreign scents that may interfere with your sense and wear natural fibers; cotton, wool, silk, etc. So I became more knowledgeable in witchcraft but the ways of old were only known by name and even then only a few of them.*

*This energy you can tap into and use," she told me. "Every object contains a certain type of energy, even after it has been harvested. This is why some spells call for specific plants and minerals, sometimes prepared in exacting ways and portions, like a recipe for cooking.*

*Kathleen also taught me to fight and embrace that part of myself which was warrior, and she taught me how to combine the two -- to meld witchcraft and fighting to draw out energy into me, to give me strength, speed and spatial awareness of what is around me; honing that skill so that I could even block other moves when I couldn't see them, to anticipate and counter. She took me out with swords and taught me to use that form of fighting and to use the staff, to look about my environment and use what was at hand as an improvised weapon. So in this way my sister was my first teacher. She taught me to be both witch and warrior, but the most important thing she taught me was to let go and to let my instincts guide me. She taught me to clear my thoughts and trust my true nature for aid. She taught me woodcraft; how to walk in the woods silently, leaving little or no trace of my passage. On those strolls as she would call them, we often were content to say nothing for hours. Sometimes she would talk. She would point out a plant or a tree and mention its uses. Like if you take the leaves of mulberry and pound it into a juice, it is helpful in light poisonings of aconite. Mixed with vinegar it's good for burns. And the berries make a nice wine. It does, we made some. Though the fermentation process takes a long time. Moonwart, pounded into a mash and placed over wounds helps, but for too long, and so it went.*

*Here be the lesson ... we are all owned in one way or another by our past. We strive to overcome those wounds, yet the harder we try, the more we pick, scratch and re-open those wounds, never letting them heal. But if we simply let go we can learn to exist within the present -- for that is where we are meant to live -- in the here and now. I didn't learn to stand up for myself until much later. In this, I was a bad student. Live by your true nature, devoid of that which has come before. Embrace all aspects of the Self, for only then can you become a whole person. To deny any part of who and what you are is to live half a life. Be honest with yourself -- only then can you unlock your full potential."*

With the marriage of John's mother and father eventually deteriorated to the point where divorce was inevitable, John's mother turned to drinking ever more. For John, this was a double-edged sword and one that he did not know how to wield well since no one had trained him. He had only the hatred he felt for his father at this point, a man he had divorced in his own mind, in fact, as well as a virtually absentee mother. Thus, John needed and sought guidance. He knew there were powers within him; something that needed to express itself in the greater world around him, but, being ignorant of the methods of the Old Ways, he was stifled. Fortune smiled upon John and reunited him for a while with his beloved sister, Kathleen, who had learned magic from their mother and fighting skills from the Army. This older sister became a master to his novice and taught him that the world around him was not a dead string of suburban houses and office buildings; not a whirr of automobiles and television sets. Kathleen preached that the world was alive and that Gods inhabited every flowing stream, each fluttering leaf and every shoot that broke the earth in the Spring – magic was everywhere. It was just a matter of how to summon it, shape it and cast it ...

And so the world came alive for the young John – the natural world anyway. The world of the "towns" with their incessant hums of tires on pavement and their nasty bickering between parents and the futility of watching his mother drink herself into the hospital – as well as the horrors that he suffered at the hands of Wayne -- was the opposite of everything he wanted in this world. He was an avowed creature of Nature and sought to tap into that source of energy, as humanity had been trying to do since Humanity first sat around a crackling fire of sticks and saw the Moon pass through the sky, since Humanity took that first step from the tangible to the abstract by uttering a sound that had meaning, when man began to name the world around him. John was looking for the same primal experience of feeling the dirt under his feet, wind rushing over his bare skin as he absorbed the flowing power of the universe and tried to, as he put it, "shape" and "direct" it to his will.

John knew he was still raw, still in need of mentoring, an acolyte, a novice at best. His mother had shown him the symbols and tools of the Craft; she had been his introduction, but, given her drinking and her unstable relationships with men, she was unable to nurture the powers of her son, who had indeed been born with many powerful omens to bear, from the date of his birth to the caul that draped over him. His sister, Kathleen, would become his dearest friend, protector and – perhaps most important – his greatest teacher of the Craft:

27

*Kathleen and I often walked to the forest that bordered my father's property. Some of it belonged to him but the majority did not. Being far from the coast, there were hills, rocks, and streams. The nearest town was over 8 miles away, so we were in the rural area, but not exactly too far from civilization. It was enough outside the city that nature held on by tooth and nail, but just barely. Even so, we took refuge there and sometimes we could get away deep enough to find the innocence we looked for, undisturbed by the hum of tires on asphalt roads or tractors in the field.*

*One day in July, we took such an excursion walking, talking, and sometimes remaining silent; going from one patch of blackberry bushes to another. It was summer. I was 14. She had just turned 20 and we had all the time in the world. After stopping for lunch, we had packed up and we took our return trip by taking another route, breaking new trails just to see what we would find.*

*Exiting the undergrowth, we came to a broad clearing, dappled with sunlight and silent. Partially buried in the leaves of the past autumns we saw a rack of antlers were sticking up. I immediately was drawn to this curiosity. Kathleen by my side, I reached to pick it up, but she grabbed my arm. Shaking my head, she said, "No that belongs to Herne and if you want it, you have to trade something you value for it." The tone in her voice told me this was important, so we left it there and continued on our way back. She told me Herne was the god of the forest and animals who lived there. Herne's symbol was the stag as well as the bull, a now-extinct bull called an auroch. He is also called Herne the Hunter, and by other names. The druids called him Hu Gadarn and others called him Cernunnas.*

*I listened and learned but Kathleen usually left me wanting more and forced me to search out more answers. She told me about other gods and goddesses, some Celtic, some Germanic, and some Norse. "Blood calls to blood." We are the children of the Gods and, as such, Gods in our own rite yet to mature into our full potential. When we pray or do rituals, we honor them but do not bow down to worship them. I absorbed this. She continued to explain to me that all religions, once stripped of the trappings of man, society and various influences are, for the most the same, except each group of people carry their own distinctive understanding and connection to their teaching, religion and beliefs. "Blood calls to blood."*

*She also said that that when stripped of all the ignorant culturalisms and trappings of man, society and such that for the most part all religions are the same. They are the path to spiritual evolution and enlightenment. Except each group of people carry their distinctive understanding and connection to their ancient beliefs. "Blood calls to blood." Kathleen would often say that the reason why the world was so screwed up was because we have removed ourselves from nature or the Natural World. We have forgotten that we are not removed from nature but a part of it. Natural law is as true for us as any creature. The Natural order trumps the laws and customs born of the sick civilization that has been created and foisted on us by generations of demented individuals.*

*Nature's rules. That was the lesson she taught me. Strip man from all technology of the day and man is only one species among many. Clever perhaps, but certainly not top dog without tool and weapon. I pondered those things after she left. Yet my mind kept returning to the antlers out in the woods. I wanted them but knew I needed a suitable trade for them. Something of value. But what? For weeks I thought about it, going through my stuff trying to come up with something a God would find acceptable in trade. I couldn't ask Kathleen. Asking my father was useless, so I had to find my own way in all of this. By the end of July I had my choice.*

*It was the first Sunday of August. I had packed a lunch, got my trading gift, grabbed my bow and arrows and machete and headed off into the woods. It took me about 2 hours to reach a clearing, and I was sweating. My canteen was half full and warm even though I had put some ice into it. The clearing was warm and dappled with sunlight shining through the trees, as I approached the reason for my visit, pulling the dog collar from my pocket (my dog died after being run over by a car some months before) it had been a good dog -- though rather stupid. It was not my first one, but the one I had all to myself my though.*

*Standing over the deer skull and antlers, I began to reach for them but then the world changed around me. The sky began to darken as if suddenly storm clouds had blocked the sun. A once calm day became windy and the hairs on my arms and head rose as if lightning was about to strike. The swaying boughs of trees began to call me, saying one name in a breathy sigh. This name was Herne, extending out into one long sound; the warmth was sucked from the air as last autumn's leaves were picked up to be blown away and float about. A crash from the brush startled me and I looked just in time to see a buck break from the undergrowth, along the same game trail my sister and I had first entered this clearing upon. It bounded past me, almost arm's length away, as I stood frozen, rooted at that spot. Now slightly frightened, I dropped the collar and grabbed the antlers, lifting them. No sooner had I touched them and the chaos began to subside, returning the world to a hot, sunny August day where hardly a breeze stirred the air. I looked around, still feeling the charge in the air, but everything else was gone, not even the sound of the buck bounding down the trail could be heard.*

29

*My hands still shaking, I cleaned off the skull and antlers as I left the clearing, heading back to more familiar lands. Once back on my own property, or leased land owned by my father, I felt I had to build it, my altar. I had to do this. I chose a place near an oak tree; high up on the branches grew the mistletoe we collected at Christmas/Yule. I started piling up stones, two of them, making these piles to support small, straight limbs and branches. Using some kudzu vine, I lashed them together to make a platform roughly two or 3 feet by about 5 feet long and three feet high. Using a sapling and for a pole, I placed the skull and antlers behind my newly made altar. Cutting my hand, I swore a blood oath that day, dedicating myself to Herne, to the Old Ways and the Gods of My Ancestors. I still bear the scar of my swearing, a scar I acknowledge proudly. For all the years I've walked this path, while I've studied the religions, I've never once strayed from my path.*

*Years later I would realize several things about that day. The first thing was the date on which I found the skull was one on which there was a full Moon that would rise that night. The day I went back for the skull and antlers was also Lughnassa, a Sabbath celebrating the harvest, First Harvest. And finally, there was a realization that took me even longer to reason out -- that the trade I made wasn't my dog's collar but me. I swore that oath on that day even before I touched the antlers sticking out from the leafy ground. Herne had laid claim to me as gods take what they will for their gifts. And I had been more aware and knowledgeable of the Gods, I would have known this. I doubt I would've done anything different.*

*This, while not truly the start of my journey, is where the journey began for me, actively seeking the knowledge. What frustrated me the most was the lack of information. I started my search in the school library, but the very thing I found on the topic of witchcraft was mainly about the Salem witchcraft trials -- and that was historically incomplete and slanted, of course, toward Christianity when it came to the religion. There was nothing on the Pagan beliefs. I sort floundered in ignorance. This is not to say I didn't have some understanding of the basics. I had seen my mother perform spells, and had been to a total of three Sabbaths; but this was years and years ago, and being so young at the time, I hadn't paid much attention to it. So, in those early days, I worked by instinct and felt it foreign to me. I crafted charms for nature using bones, stakes, vines and plants. I made up rituals on the spur of the moment. I called upon Herne, Morrigan, Lugh of the Long Hand, Odin, Freya, the names my sister had told me. The days passed into weeks, into months, seasons changed and life went on. Things changed as they always do.*

*When I found my altar broken up, I was beyond angry. My father had remarried and moved away from the house and property. My sister Jean and her boyfriend Frank had moved in. Jean had become Christian, mostly in name, but anything not Christian was looked down upon. This is most likely due to the incidents of violence between her and our mother before the divorce, which was one of the reasons for my sisters going with my father way back when. So I moved my altar deeper into the woods off my father's property.*

*Returning to the clearing where I had first encountered the power of Herne, I went about constructing my sanctuary. I took a wooden lattice that was lying around and, using poles, I had cut down, created an enclosure. Having nailed the lattice to the polls, I went in search for blackberry bushes small enough to transplant. Digging them up, carrying them back and replanting them on the outside of the enclosure took a while. Once completed, I was satisfied that once they grew, it would cover the sanctuary in a circular hedge.*

*Once I had a safe place for my altar, I rebuilt it, but this time I would do it a little differently. The enclosure was an octagon shape measuring roughly 20 feet across. The posts were set at each cardinal point and halfway between them in the north-north-east section, I put a door using baling wire for hinges and a rope to secure it. In the north part, I built my altar, transporting the rocks from the old site most of the way in a wheelbarrow, and then in a sack the rest of the way. I had to cut new branches and kudzu vine for the top. The charms and talismans I had made before were repaired and hung about on the inside lattice wall. In the east, south and west points, I made a small altar of stone (later I would learn the names of these – cairns). In the center I built a small fire-pit ringed in stones of quartz. Rummaging through some of the things my father had left in the house, I found a wooden salad bowl and amber glass goblet -- and a few other things I brought to the sanctuary. I made a pentacle by weaving green branches and placing it in the antlers. I cut my hand again, smearing blood on all that I had in there. "Blood calls to blood." Then I prepared to hold my first ritual.*

*The wood for the first fire was the branches I had used for the first altar. I collected this and clay from the ground, which was everywhere in Orange County (probably where it got its name from). I made crude bowls and placed them on the three cairns, placing in them fire to the south, hot coals and put powdered herbs on them in the east, and water in the west. I soon learned that I should have used metal bowls or fired the clay, but live and learn. The bowl with the water leaked. The one with fire, using some lighter fluid as fuel, cracked and caused the entire cairn to burn with flames. The bowl in the east, though, dried out and cracked; it worked well enough. If you choose to do this, I might suggest using metal woks; this will give you the sturdy material to remain safe in performing rituals.*

*After correcting this problem, I had to once again regain the level of expertise at which I desired to perform a ritual of re-dedication of my ritual space. Now, I should point out that this was done over the span of two months. It was getting close to time when holding an outdoor ritual would have been uncomfortable, even with clothes. So, I was a bit pressed for time. In these early days, I did everything by instinct and never wrote anything down. The idea of keeping a journal or Book of Shadows was utterly unknown to me, so there is no accurate record of this ritual, except by my memory. Such as it is, I will try to recall as much of it as I can here so you can judge for yourself by my actions:*

*I brought with me one of the swords my father had purchased while stationed in Germany. With this I drew a circle in the earth I had raked bare of leaves within the enclosure.*

*I draw a circle around, shutting out the world of man. May nothing pass it from within or without, lest I grant permission and welcome it to do so. "By my will it is done."*

*At the East Cairn I drew a pentagram in the earth, rapping the sore blade on the stones.*

*"I call upon the Eastern Gate. Open! Bear witness and aid me in my rite."*

*I followed this formula, changing it slightly at each direction, having already placed incense (dried herbs), fire, water and fresh earth and moss at each point.*

*Standing now before the altar and the northern part I placed three fingers on the head of the deer skull... "Herne, hear my call, and be welcomed in my rite!" Removing my fingers, raising my sword point skyward, I said, "Hear me Gods of Old. Blood calls to blood. Here be a place made sacred on my sweat and blood, and be welcomed."*

*I made a small cut on my hand, waving it about fast to cast the blood, small amount that it was, around that space.*

*"Grant me the blessings I seek! Guide me in my journey. Give me the wisdom to know all things, the cunning to use it, and the strength and courage to overcome all obstacles!"*

*I picked up a piece of burning wood out of the central fire pit, touched it to my left wrist. "By blood, by steel and now fire, I forever seal myself to the Old Ways. So Mote It Be!"*

*I then ended the ritual by dumping the earth on top of coals on the Eastern Cairn and the water onto the flames of the Southern Cairn. Once cool enough to move both of these, I went to douse the fire of the central fire pit. Once I was sure the fires were fully out, I left; got my bike and went home. Since this moment, I've never once wavered, never hid what I believed, and I have gained much knowledge and wisdom.*

*Today with paganism, there are those who have hardly committed themselves. They often take up the mantle of the craft with little thought and set it aside just as quickly. I've often pondered this, and I have come to the conclusion that they do so because they need not sacrifice to join. Pagans greet the seekers with open arms, with trust not earned; regard their commitment as honest and sincere without testing. In Wicca, the Initiator says to the person seeking entry into the coven at their first-degree initiation "O Thou who standeth on the threshold between the pleasant worlds of free man and the Dread domains of the Lords of the Outer Spaces, hast Thou the courage to make the assay?" The Postulant confirms the answer to the Initiator, who places the point of a blade over their heart and says, "For Thou verily it were for you better to rush on my blade and perish then make the attempt with fear in your heart." And the reply to give is the password to gain entry. (This is taken from Janet and Stewart far as book A Witch's Bible: a Complete Witch's Handbook). There is little or no testing, no probationary period etc., for many covens. To those I have had contact with I suggest this to them: test them, make conditions that must be met, get to know the person and make them wait a year and a day (minimum) before you initiate them. At least in this manner those you bring into your coven will be vetted, and most likely will stick with it.*

*Even so, where's the sacrifice? We call them Gods and Goddesses; we invoke their names, seek their blessings, but for the most part we do not understand them. In these modern times, they have been sanitized, cleaned up to fit our idea of revised history. I've witnessed covens calling upon Morrigan, the Battle Crow, yet did not understand the terrible nature of this Goddess; or seek to gain a God of Macha, one of the triple aspects of the Goddess Morrigan, who would weave spells using the blood of the slain. Badb, another of Morrigan's aspects, decided the fate of men and battles; or Nemon, the crone who would harvest the dead of battles. In their tidy modern mind, they would call Her to a ritual that has little to do with her nature. In Welsh lands the Morriga were summoned on the eve of battle. Morrigan was a Quint of Goddesses. Morrigan, Fea, Nemon, Badb and Macha provide magic to help defeat their enemies, part of which was to encourage warriors to the level of battle-madness, berserkers was the common term for them.*

*They would invoke Cernunnos, and, while the God of Nature, he is also known to be associated with the God of the Underworld. It would be better to call upon Dagda for the God and Danu for the Goddess, as these are more in keeping with the modern conception of Wicca, at least for those following the Irish tradition. Enough, if you prefer more lusty aspects try Llud for the God and Druantia Goddess.*

*My point here is the Old Gods are not the neat and clean deities most see them as. Nature's not some gentle summer afternoon in the park; it is a battle of survival, a match of wills; it is as much life as it is death. We are by our very natures Children of these Gods and "Blood calls to blood." Make small sacrifices, gain insight, and learn that without it your commitment is less than it would be with it. There are no grocery stores in the primeval forest. Learn that true commitment means sacrifice and without it your deeds will win you naught. With it, all there is awaits you."*

Committed as he was to this Path of his, having shed his Blood and summoned the ancient Gods of Nature, and having made a trade that turned out to be his very essence (perhaps his Soul), John never seemed to find his place in the world of Modern Times. He had purposefully tried to hearken back to an Old time when heroes like Llud lured red and white dragons to their deaths on May Day to save his people; a time when men swore blood oaths to each other and made them real by their actions; a time when the Ogham alphabet was a series of symbols deriving their meaning from the trees that sprouted from the earth of Ireland, not monikers taken from the Christian Bible. He believed in the force of the individual's will to create a reality for himself, and so he tried to do that for himself, just as he had conjured the spirit of Herne that day in the woods.

The world around him – a place filled with a drunken mother, a cruel and distant father, abusive and perverted elders, foster homes, state hospitals and schools that did not have the kind of knowledge he desired – did not understand John during his teenage years. When he spoke of swords, fighting with a staff, hand-to-hand combat and Gods who looked over warriors with psychologists and counselors, they saw this not as another, very necessary step in his Path, but as defiant, anti-social behavior from a misguided, dysfunctional kid who needed more therapy. He was moved from foster home to foster home, from one institution to another and at one point to a state-run hospital because of what the State deemed problems that were more serious than a foster setting could handle. All of these artificial settings were bad enough on their own, but then they separated him even further from the Nature that he needed to work his Magick, as well as the tools of his Craft.

John did not see his father for years, having cast him off years earlier after attempting to see him by escaping form the "boys' Home." His mother, too, was wild and could be abusive, especially of the two sisters. Her brain was addled by booze and her Soul was wracked by the violence of her relationship with the father. Thus, John set out to find meaning on his own, to find Wisdom. The revelation of the truth, true Wisdom, is the one common goal of all seekers, especially the Pagan who casts off the shell of Modern Society and tramps down a path of his/her own. Just as he and his sister had broken new trails through the woods that lined his father's land, John was about to spend his late teen years and early twenties forging his own Path in the world. There would be little of the trappings of Modernity for John. He floated from place to place. He stayed with his father for a couple of years and then was remanded to another institution, where it was determined that – again – his "problems" were too great for the institution to handle. He stopped going to school, even though he was finishing the curriculum way ahead of his peers. The teachers didn't know how to handle him, either.

*"I started to skip school on a regular basis within the first grading period of eighth grade I had completed the math book in science except for the labs and was almost done reading the history textbook. My teachers led by Mr. Hicks who was actually educated as a PE teacher of working as a math teacher and sports coach felt it best that I stay with the class I should point out that a year prior to this and another school district I spent all of 27 days in the sixth grade before being promoted to the seventh grade. I honestly believe had these so called educators at the CW Stanford junior high school had allowed me to advance at my own pace clearly a pace that far exceeded that of the common denominator with in the class I may have graduated high school in short order and got me a scholarship to a number of universities in the area or UNC chapel hill being the closest two. Yet instead they stifled me, berated my unorthodox approach to math even though I still came up with the right answer and constricted my absorption of knowledge to what was in the textbook. Columbus was not the first European to sail to the Americas. Leif Ericson predated him by some 500 plus or minus years before. Yes there are some rather unresolved issues here. Yet it was this that went and continued to push me down a path of self destruction ... no one event can be*

*said to make or break a person's life, yet they can drastically alter future events in such a way as to seem so."*

The psychologists wanted to blame it all on syndromes, such as Parental Alienation Syndrome and the long-term effects of not having a relationship with those who had been close to him. Doctors tried to label the anger that welled up in him when he was confronted; they tried to pigeonhole the explosions of violence that sprang from him. They slapped typical labels on it: "poor impulse control" and "low frustration tolerance."

But what if that wasn't the answer?

What if John's Soul was a different Soul that had tapped into something that could not be so easily defined and regulated? Maybe it was a deeper well with deeper waters that ran back to the ancient, holy soil of Ireland and Wales where stone cairns still dot the hill tops and mark the movements of the sun so that druids, to this day, can track the solstice and celebrate another Sabbath? What if his Soul had truly been – however unwittingly – "marked," as he says, by Herne, that ferocious God of the Stag on that day he traded for the antlers? What if Ogham and the runes were his language and he could find those Magickal combinations of sounds that created incantations and spells? The doctors labeled him as Antisocial, as one who "engaged in behaviors that were against the values of society and the rules of society." Then again, John came from a long line of folks who had wandered away from persecution and the "rules of society." With that blood in his veins, and the blood calling to his blood, John wandered off after being locked up at the age of seventeen and he set out on His Path to find what the Universe had in store for him:

*"The dedicated seekers' first duty is to seek out knowledge and understanding. These things cannot be separate because by themselves they are incomplete. For knowledge is dangerous as it is the skilled hand without direction. The reverse of this, wisdom without knowledge, is the traveler without the clear route and not the right skills to arrive at the proper destination. The story of the tortoise and the hare comes to mind, slow and steady wins the race. In this age of instant gratification, most do not have the patience to travel the path of the dedicated seeker. They are like the child who wants what they see now and if it is not forthcoming, they pout. To have ice cream one first needs to finish the meal. To have a meal, it must be prepared; before that they must kindle the fire, before that the plants must grow and the beast must be hunted; before that they must learn to grow the plants and to hunt the beast. And all this begins at the feet of a teacher, listening and learning. My teachers were gone, both of them not in my*

*life. I was alone with only basic concepts of what I needed to learn without having it before me to study.*

*I searched for information which brought me to the public library. I should point out as a male teenager I was not a bookworm, though I was not illiterate either. But the books I kept running into in the public library sided strongly with the Christian stance on witchcraft. Then I found the section called New Age. Okay, I admit it: I read and read, struggling through volume after volume of some of the worst drivel I have ever read. I was just about to give up when I ran across a book on developing one's psychic potential. I checked the book out and, whenever I could be by myself, read this book cover to cover.*

*In one lesson there was how to focus your concentration. I would practice and practice this all the time. As it only involved me and finding a focal point, it was an exercise I could do pretty much anywhere. Unfortunately I tended to do this a lot and realized there is a drawback to doing anything too much... this being you get too good at it and tend to slip easily into that mode even when don't intend to do so. Like in school, watching television while being lectured for "daydreaming" in class by your parents. "Huh? What? Could you repeat the question?" A phrase that generally doesn't go over well with a father who believes his son should hang on his every word and tends to get angry when he doesn't. Yeah, sure. I could have explained it to him but he would have said something like, "Focus on your damned school work." Though, if he said that I could have told him that I had already completed my math, science and history textbooks within the first grading periods as the material was simple, but they wouldn't promote me or place me in Advanced Placement classes. But I felt there was no point to it. My solution to this... simply not to go to school. I wasn't learning anything so there was little point in it.*

*That choice left me plenty of time to read and practice my techniques. It was around April or May of 1982 while sitting on a large rock out in the woods that I had an experience that amazed me, filled me with a terrible sense of awe and scared the shit out of me at the same time.*

*In one of the books I was reading it discussed a technique of reaching out with your mind. I think the chapter was called Psychic Touch or Psychic Awareness or something to that effect. This chapter led me to trying to perceive the world around me by focusing my consciousness outward to touch that which I was using as my focal point.*

*Now I had done this countless times, more than I could even give count to. Sometimes I tried to do it for a minute or two, sometimes for a half an hour.*

*All of it was an utter failure. I would get frustrated and give up even though the book specifically said that I shouldn't. Yet I always felt I was on the verge of something. Even so, I was on the verge of just giving up. I should say there's another term for determination, which is stubbornness, and I kept trying.*

*I found myself out on that flat rock worn smooth on top, relaxing, doing my breathing exercises and focusing on the tree in front of me. I closed my eyes and tried to reach out with my conscious mind and try to feel the texture of the bark. I began around noon, maybe a little after, breathing in through my nose and out of my mouth. I had done this for so long that by this time it came natural to me. Time moved on yet at some point I became unaware of its passage. The sounds of the woods around me faded, each noise falling off one by one as I pushed myself outward to try to touch the tree, narrowing my focus down further and further until there was nothing in my awareness but me, my breathing and the desire to make contact with that tree. It was then that something clicked.*

*One instant I was there within myself and the next it was as if I were everywhere. A rush of sensations flooded into me. I was the squirrel scampering along a branch, my nails scraping on the bark, gripping its surface as I chose another. A bird on a limb, my feet grasping it, ready to spring and spread my wings. Insects moving, following scents along a trail, worms moving through soil, myself sitting on the rock but with only a sense of weariness I was not accustomed to. I felt other sensations, a multitude of them; hunger, cool wind through fur or maybe feathers, warmth, a sense of movement, many thing touching me along my frame and touching something. Almost as soon as it happened I recoiled in shock, frightened. Just like that, it was gone. I was me, only me, within me. Though some of the disorientation faded quickly, my body felt as if it weighed hundreds of pounds. I looked up and saw a pair of squirrels upon a limb a few trees away. One let out a chittering squeak of what sounded like alarm and ran, leaping to another tree, soon followed by the second. At the same time a handful of birds took flight as if they were startled too.*

*My mouth was dry and my tongue was stuck to the roof of my mouth. My body felt like it had gone to sleep and now the pain of restored blood flow struck like millions of needles stuck into my skin. Gingerly, I moved my arm and looked at my watch seeing the digital display reading just after four in the afternoon. Confused, wondering where the time had gone, I sat in the damp ground with my back against the rock. When I could move with some measure of normalcy I stood up and made my way home. Not all that sure exactly what had just happened. The books I had gotten the exercise from didn't mention anything about this. And, of course, I didn't have anyone to ask. I decided not to do that exercise again, but then did, much later. However, not with any success. Finally, I gave upon it. Being fifteen and a male, I became interested in other things, namely girls.*

*It was soon after this that my relationship with my father turned from strained to hostile. The incident that happened on that rock began a slow change in my consciousness and it was these changes that began to allow me to see the world and the people in it in the stark reality that it is. With this gloss stripped away, they became dull and crude, with very little in their character to raise them up above my own status... or so it appeared. In this state, their words lost meaning, the convoluted system of laws, social standards, culture and such began to look arbitrary and capricious. What is considered human morality seemed to run counter to everything I saw going on. In this, I was introduced to the hypocrisy of humanity as a whole.*

*My life started to become more complex with the introduction of my father's new girlfriend and soon to be wife (a practice find to be antiquated and serving no real purpose except to ritualize a commitment under the guise and sanctity of religious morality turned legally binding contractual obligation). With my new and still evolving insight into the world around me and the dross of the status quo and accompanying rigors removed from my mind I found it unacceptable to blindly follow much less accept the pseudo- authority of this woman who was neither blood related nor of such caliber to be granted my respect. Especially when I saw it for what it was, an attempt to exert her own dominance within the family structure, to create her own sense of place and status while assuring obedience to her own desires. Of course, I couldn't put all this into words then, but instinctively I knew it for what it was and rebelled against it.*

*I spent more time away from home, seeking the peaceful isolation of the woods. There I felt complete, whole. I didn't need to be bogged down by the conventions of society with its false politeness and judgmental stares of people. It was during this time that I also began seeing the patterns of life. Not the cycle of birth, life, death and rebirth. No, that was already known to me. I refer here to how life is more often than not a mere chance, causes and reactions, a single act can create a series of events that cascade and disrupt the surrounding forest and the animals that dwell there. It struck me at that moment that this is how Witchcraft works: like a minor sound rebounds off surfaces sending its vibrations throughout the snow and ice until it gives way to come roaring down in an avalanche. I recalled something Kathleen has said: "Magic, by whatever name it goes, is the act of exerting your will to create change. That act is done in a ritualized manner to assist the witch to focus on the intent more clearly." It also came to me that all of humanity, or at least the vast majority, are all merely caught up in their own reactionary trap, that they are all reacting to what has*

39

*come before, playing this vast game of tag in a chain reaction reaching far back into time when that first moment of Primary Action happened. Ever since then, it has been a game of billiards with infinite numbers of balls on the table in motion.*

*I didn't stay very long in the house after my soon-to-be step-mother and my father moved in together. Then they sought to take the family to the World's Fair in Knoxville, Tennessee. I declined, hoping to be left at the house; but, instead, they placed me with my oldest sister, Jean. Well, as it happened, Frank and Jean, being chronic marijuana users, Frank accused me of stealing loose change from an ashtray. I hadn't and professed my innocence. Yet, Jean, the loyal girlfriend and disloyal sister, took Frank's side in this. Angry, fed up and totally alone I made up my mind I was not going to stay where I was obviously unwanted. That night, I stole Frank's car, his prized Pontiac Trans Am and drove it halfway across the state to visit my mother. It was purely an act of retaliation and, at the time, it felt liberating and very satisfying – though it was short lived.*

*Within 36 hours I was arrested and put in jail. The next day I was transferred to Orange County Jail where I sat until I was released to the custody of my father. To be honest they may as well have left me in jail. I was a thief, branded and condemned. Fine. I was sent a few weeks later to a halfway house run by the Lutheran Church for teens where I stayed for next three months. Gods, it was great. Well, except for the church every Sunday. Why is it, do you think, that all church-sponsored charities have as a part of its "help" religion? As if it this magic (don't laugh) wand they can wave over the afflicted to make it all better? They would be served better to talk to the people they are trying to help to get to know them instead of force-feeding them their ideology and philosophy like geese are fed on a farm.*

*For my "transgressions" I was told to pay restitution of 300 dollars and the cost of the court, the official charge was "Unauthorized Use of Motor Conveyance", but the charge would be deferred (meaning not to go to trial for a conviction) and have one year of probation.*

*Over those three months at the halfway house I enjoyed myself. There were seven of us there and I was the only male. I had just turned 16, was good looking and had more personal confidence than a person of that age should have. Bed hopping at night was not unheard of, not just for me. Sly grins at breakfast and snickers abounded. I see today programs on television of teens having sex and the adults act so shocked and outrage. Just another act of hypocrisy. For they were doing it themselves. How else do they do they have a teen son or daughter and they are barely past thirty? The only difference is technology; it's more open and easy. Biology will override artificial morality any time.*

However, it was in the city that I came across my first Pagan/Occult books store. I was in awe of the crystals, herb selection and books. Jewelry was a bit of a disappointment, all of it looked too feminine for my tastes, though I couldn't afford any of it anyway. The daggers were a huge draw, or if you wish, athames. They even had a few swords. Runes cut into colorful stones, dozen or so different types of Tarot decks; the list goes on and on. But, as I've said, I didn't actually have the money to buy anything. That irked me. Here were some of the very things I had been searching for well over a year and all I could do was look at it. Everything was expensive and had I had the money I would have gladly spent it all there. "One of everything please." But without the funds I was a very frustrated kid looking through the window of the candy store... I settled on getting one book from the store. That book, recommended by the owner, was called The Complete Book of Saxon Witchcraft by Raymond Buckland, or something like that. It was a long time ago.

While growing up with my mother I had some information imparted to me that I had not found particularly strange; it was just normal. However, with book in hand, I came to see some similarities in what my mother had done were really minor acts of Witchcraft. It also came to my attention that a lot of people reacted negatively to my having the book. From the Lutheran employees of the halfway house in particular. But that was fine as I only needed to be there until January.

Was it because of that book that I was taken from the halfway house a bit early? Who can say? At the time I felt it was. I later found that it had been the plan of my father all along to send me to John Umstead Hospital, a state mental institution. Problems at the house had to be because there was something wrong with me; it certainly couldn't be anything to do with him (though both of his daughters had left home by 16 years old and he was on his third marriage). So after the holiday season I was shipped up to the loony bin due to my "emotional and behavioral problems."

"The Crazy House", the "Nut House", call it what you will. In truth, it was where people are sent who do not fit in with society's ideal of "normal." Or where people with money send their kids when they no longer have the time to figure out why they act the way they do. Have to say, it is interesting people you finds in these places. They had sections for people as young as six all the way up to adults. I was in the adolescent ward/unit for long-term care. I was handed over to a therapist named Ann, mainly because she was young and good-looking and males of my age would better be manipulated to "open up" to her. And they were right, to a point. Sixteen years old with a female in her mid-twenties looking as good as she did, I wanted her to like me, perhaps impress her. Though at first, I

41

*was not exactly forthcoming with information. Even after I had relaxed a little bit I was still not spilling my guts to her. If the truth be known, I was biding my time, waiting to reach my 18th birthday so when I left I could be on my own – free.*

*Outside of this, I was the oldest male on the floor which ranged from as young as 12 or 13. Opposite our wing was the girls' wing, same age group. They, the minders called 'Health care Technicians', kept us separate for most of the time. Having just come from a place where having sex was like a recreational period, this place was like a monastery in comparison. And although I gave chase, my success at finding companionship was not all that great. There were two girls in particular I was rather drawn to. Tina and Beth. I have often thought of tracking them down but never have.*

*My pursuit of girls was less successful than my pursuit of knowledge was. I pored over books I had and while a good deal of it rang true, some things just didn't fit. I used the rituals and the spells in the books and met with some success... and some failures. Yet, each time, be they successes or failures, it was a struggle. The need to be exact in spells and rituals threw off my rhythm, my words faltered; the process was hasty at best. There was no flow in it, no spontaneity. Now I'm not saying what is contained in that book or others is bad, or they don't work. What I am saying is that we are all individuals and that the energy flows uniquely for each of us. Because of this each of us must seek to understand how the power and you react and interact with each other. In groups this is different because acting as a single mind and in synchronicity is important; thus the group needs to be harmonized, each individual coming together to support and strengthen the whole. More on this later, for now I will focus on the single practitioner.*

*The more I tried these formulas in the book, the more I realized they didn't fit me. At first the "minders" wouldn't let us outside unsupervised due to the high probability of run-aways; however, being who and what I am, I was able to manipulate them into trusting me out by myself. Not to mention that I had found a master key to the locks inside the hospital. I had copies made and was able to come and go as I pleased. Frustrated and needing time to myself I went into the woods beyond the baseball field across the street from the ward. There, surrounded by the pines common there, I started to walk. This is how I had always been. Nature had always given me strength and solace. With each step along the game trails I became more myself. Comfortable, relaxed, happy. Content, I began to run. Not that I had anywhere I needed to be. I did so because I wanted to. The more I ran the more my mind cleared of the clutter of civilization. The animals around this patch of woods were not startled by my passing, but simply noticed my passing. I was merely another one of them. Not a danger to them, I wasn't hunting. Certainly not with the amount of noise I was making. Circling back around I came to a clearing and stopped. The area was dead silent, eerily so. Where before the sights and sounds of the wild life had been present, there were none. Below, the earth seemed to vibrate beneath my feet in a steady hum. All this made me pull up short and stop.*

*Slowly, cautiously, I walked into the clearing and as I approached the center the sensations became stronger. I had only felt this twice before. Once in the clearing where the deer antlers had laid. Before that was on one of the trips my mother and I would take "ghost hunting," specifically the one trip my mother, Stanley and I went on after the divorce of my parents. That was at a place outside of a place called Pittsboro/Silver City called "Devil's Stomping Grounds." That first time I had been a little kid and wasn't allowed to go into the circle, but now, in that place in the woods, I did.*

*Reaching the center of the nearly perfect circle of a clearing, where nothing grew, that same vibration flowed around me, no longer contained in the earth, it reached up into the air. Deep in my bones, as if standing in front of a huge speaker, it sank deep and pulsated along my skin and it caressed me as it hummed and throbbed. The hairs along my arms stood up and I felt the disorienting sensation of being in more than one place. As if in the clearing, I was not precisely in this world. It was a strange but wonderful feeling and I let it wash over me and through me. With an urge to do so, I began to spin around, letting my arms extend from my sides as I turned round and round with the joy of it all. When I stopped, words came from within me, unbidden they sprang, without the conscious thoughts needed to formulate them:*

*"I stand at the borders of Dark and Light*
*In the Land of Mist and Snow*
*I am Power Incarnate*
*Neither Spirit nor Flesh*
*I walk the Way in Between*
*Outside, yet always within*
*I am All Things, Nothing, yet remain always*
*Life and Death dance to my tune,*
*From beginning to end and back again*
*I fill the vessel and empty it*
*In time to fill another*
*Eternal, Forever, Never Ending, Never Beginning*
*I am that which is and one with all*
*Heed me now! Hear my words!*
*I am Master of the Ways!"*

*These words came and seemed to rebound within my mind, echoing silently but loud enough to draw out everything else. In the clearing these same words swirled around me though never passing beyond into the surrounding woods. The hum pulsated, thrumming through me like a beat of a slow drum, bass deep and full. Then more words came to me and I had to speak them:*

> *"I am the stream that flows*
> *The wind that blows*
> *The rich earth and deep snows*
> *I am the fire that warms*
> *The rage that burns*
> *The life that gives and that which takes*
> *Count me not for I am limitless*
> *To understand me is to be me*
> *To live beyond all things yet within them*
> *To name me is to limit me*
> *I have none*
> *Be within me*
> *And I shall dwell in you*
> *Embrace me*
> *And a God you shall be."*

*The words ended but continued to echo in my mind. Were they my words or were they from somewhere else? Then as suddenly as they came, all of it stopped, like it had been sucked out of the world. I heard birds and squirrels and wind in the trees. The vibrations below my feet was still there but less noticeable than before. Exhaustion swept over me as if I had been doing hard work all day long. Yet, even so, as I made my way back to the Ward I felt enlivened by all that had happened. I didn't tell anyone there about this. Sure that if I had done so they really would have looked me up, pumped me full of drugs and tossed me into a padded room somewhere as they did with some of the adults who were really crazy. To be honest, at times, I have questioned my own sanity. But now I know it's not me who is nuts but all those people running around in step to the tune and beat that others play; they have lost their own minds. The people who scurry about to and fro, always rushing and never getting anywhere. The poor souls devoid of Spirit who will never hear the names of Gods whispered through the boughs in the wind, see beyond the surface of what they call reality and see the intricate patterns of life's weaving.*

*That night my dreams were filled with many things but what stuck out the most was a theme that had been a recurring one for a long time, since I was very young...*

*Running through a forest of rich greens, grey rocks and brown bark, it is spring but snow still clung to the shadowy places among the tree trunks and stone lees. I wasn't alone. I heard them behind me and to the other side. Looking down, I saw I had no clothes on, but that was normal in this dream. The cold was there, my breath puffed out white clouds as I moved over the land. But I wasn't cold. Quite the contrary, my skin burned with heat. Ahead were other animals, prey. I could smell their rich musky scent in the air with each breath. Running and leaping over fallen trees, tiny streams of melted ice and up or around rocky outcroppings. I advanced. Now, no longer human, not on two legs but on four, I swiftly set the pace. It was nearing dark but with enough light left to see by. Under a fence we crept, feeling the rough wood rubbing along our backs. To either side of me other wolves hunted, ahead the bleating of sheep drew us on. Slowly now, we crept nearer until we were in striking distance. At that moment the wind shifted and they had our scent, in a panic they scattered away from us. Like a signal had sounded we burst forth into the chase. The rest of the pack now forgotten, with my target chosen, I focused on only that. They were fast but no match for me. Soon one fell under my teeth; jaws clamping down on a leg, breaking bones. A panicked, fearful bleating became shrill and pain-soaked. That was short-lived for my momentum carried me forward to find its throat, my teeth tearing savagely and cutting off all sounds. A pack member caught up and together we drug off the dead animal toward the fence where other wolves had a lamb and an old ram. There we began to eat, ripping into our kills. Tearing chunks of it, shearing and cracking bones, separating the bodies into more manageable pieces. Then we were off, under the fence and back into the safety of the woods.*

*The dream has been with me most of my life, not specifically this one, just the theme of the being both human and Wolf. I have always had an affinity for wolves, and while I'm a dog person to be sure, I prefer wolf hybrids over them. I, for a short time, owned two and they acted more like family than most of my real family has.*

*The days at John Umstead Hospital passed; I completed my education early and really had very little to do besides keep my therapy appointments which were ultimately of no real help to the issues I had. Though, this is probably more my fault than theirs. I kept everyone at arm's length. Perhaps one Health- tech named Ken is probably the only person I allowed some small insight but even he was kept at a distance. I don't trust easily and my friends are few. To be called a friend by me is an honor that elevates that person to a higher level than they perhaps even know. I know my trust issues stem from my past, the abuse, the betrayal, the sense I could only rely on myself. Yet, this cautious attitude has served me well because in the world the people I have encountered have, with some exceptions, let me down in one way or another. This has always left an empty place inside me because I have always desired a "family" of close friends and because of this I have frequently tried to make these connections... though they didn't last long.*

*I was in John Umstead Hospital by my choice after the first six months of my stay there because I wasn't ready to leave. Every six months I was brought before a county judge where I was asked if I was well enough to leave. Twice I said no, not because I thought I needed to stay there or I was getting any help, but because if I did leave, I would have to be under my father's roof. May of 1984 finally came and being 17 with only 5 months to go before my birthday, a diploma in hand and promises from my sister, Kathleen, to let me stay with her, her husband and her daughter far away from my father, I decided it was time to go. And so I left. One day I spent under the roof of my father and then moved to Gastonia to live with my sister and her family. I stayed there the next nine or ten months.*

*While I lived there I worked in Charlotte with my brother-in-law and saved my money. I did pay rent to them but I had no other expenses. However, not really having a job to speak of before and turning 18, the legal age to drink beer and wine at the time, I made some workplace faux-pas. For one, I went to lunch next door where I worked and had a beer with the pizza. Okay, everyone is entitled to one mistake and as I still did my job as well, I was not criticized, but what finally led me to getting let go was getting a little tipsy at the Christmas party. I should know better but I have never learned my limit with drinking, being that I spent most of my mid-teens isolated from what many teens learned by going to parties and such other rites of passage. It was probably this that made me decide to leave, but I had been feeling the need to leave for a long time.*

*While I had lived with my sister, I learned a little more about but nothing like I had before. Certainly she was knowledgeable in certain areas; she was less so in others. I realized her knowledge was more academic and from books instead of from actually experiencing them first hand, while my experiences were the sources of my knowledge. Whether it was the estranged relationship from our mother or perhaps it was due to the influences of her husband that she gravitated toward Christianity. However, it was obvious she was holding back as if she were denying that part of herself that was like me. That seemed to be something I couldn't understand. Why reject the very essence of who you are? I never got an answer to that and never will.*

*I struck out on my own. I didn't have any transportation except for my own two feet. With a duffle bag on my back I hit Interstate 85 with my thumb out. I cast a small spell and in 10 minutes had a ride all the way to New Orleans.*

*Freedom. That is what I felt standing there on the side of Interstate 85 with my thumb out. The excitement of adventure awaiting me as I walked backwards looking at the traffic coming towards me. The ride that stopped to pick me up was a Dodge van from the 1970's. Behind the wheel was a guy about mid-to-late thirties. Pleasant enough, somewhat of a Free Spirit type, though in another era he would have fit right into a flop house around Haight Ashbury in Frisco or on some commune in Northern California. He even had some weed and offered to share, though I declined. He smoked, I drove, and it worked out. It was in this way we made it to New Orleans in one day, stopping for gas, food and bathroom breaks along the way. We parted company there, me staying in the city and him continuing south to get a job on an off-shore rig.*

*I found a cheap hotel and got a room, more to have a safe place to stash my duffel bag than anything else while I explored the area. I puttered around, looking at this and that, certainly looking like a tourist as I paid attention to things that locals would normally pass by ignoring. Yeah, I'll admit it, I was gawking.*

*I especially loved the above-ground graveyards, but then I love all graveyards. Except these modern ones that have no real style, cookie cutter headstones or worse, those flush to the ground, bronze plaques that have no character of their own. No, the places I love usually have to be about 100 or more years old or more. Back when a headstone said something about the person below, a monument attesting to the life of an individual. Sadly, today we plant our loved ones in the ground and forget them, not even bothering to visit, clean up the site, or setting as marker that hales the life lived, struggles overcome; nothing but a name, some dates and as few words as possible to save money. I truly believe if it were legal many would send their dead to the landfill.*

*But I suppose the thing that struck me the most as the most remarkable was that various beliefs sit side-by-side in relative peace. Voudon and Christianity, other beliefs like European Witchcraft as well. I had never seen this. Even that Occult store I had found years before was half hidden behind the crystals, Dream Catchers and other New Age type stuff. Here they sold Voodoo dolls in the storefront window! Amazed, excited, chomping at the bit I nearly dashed through the door.*

47

*Brass bells rang as I came through the threshold and again as the door closed behind me. My senses were assaulted from every direction. Sharp but pleasant smell of sandalwood incense did battle with the overwhelming number of herbs and other ingredients from Pufferfish to Zomia. Pre-packaged "grave-dirt" – though I think this was more for the tourist types, along with the Voodoo dolls. Two customers were in the store with me. Each there separately, you can tell that. The woman behind the counter looked up, raised an eyebrow and then went back to "neutral-faced" that most small store owners get, smiling only when you actually bring something up to the counter to ring up. The other person in the room was this really old, nearly bone and skin, white-haired woman sitting in a chair crocheting of all things. She had not looked up ignoring all presence that walked around her. If not for the crocheting, I might have mistaken her for a display.*

*As I walked around the shop I could feel their secretive glances on me, I thought it was because I was new or perhaps white in a Voodoo shop, though I found out that this isn't at all rare – a white guy in a Voodoo shop. I found out what was remarkable was that I was white deep inside the area called Algiers in 1985 and had not been accosted, robbed or anything.*

*I was looking over the candles, selecting two, a black and a red, more because I liked the color than anything and then got a pack of six tea candles which were white. I went to the counter, exchanged pleasantries with the woman behind the counter and inquired if she had any Thornapple leaves. I purchased a small bag of dried whole leaves and left.*

*I returned the next day and picked up a book, an old worn copy of Valient's Natural Magick, out of the used book rack. It was then she (the store owner) noticed my two weapons, a spring loaded three section steel baton and a dagger I wore under my jean jacket hanging upside-down from a leather tie over my shoulder. The dagger had an eight-inch blade that started out about two inched wide. Steel guard and pommel with a wooden handle. Double-edged and razor sharp. I used it in ritual and everything else. (I've never understood why people have a dagger specifically for ritual but then I am very practical. I doubt my ancestors set aside a perfectly good blade. She asked me to see the blade and noticed the runic symbols on one side and the oghamic symbols on the other.)*

*As she looked at she said, "It has tasted blood." It was a statement, so I replied, "Yes, my own."*
*She went on: "No this is death, I sense."*

*Well the leaf spring it was made from did come from a wrecked car so I told her so. I was the first owner of the blade and certainly didn't kill anyone with it; it was more of a deterrent. It was about this time the old woman spoke up, calling me 'child' and telling me to give her my hands. I did and kneeling there she closed her eyes and said, roughly, over a spread of Tarot cards before her ...*
*"Child of Air, born of water, touched by fire, you walk the earth*
*Dual is your soul, ruled by the hunter's moon*
*Legba blessed three times, the serpent lives within you*
*You will travel far, but never by waters of your birth*
*Night is your time, when you live most*
*But always trapped*
*Yes there is power in you child*
*It burns bright and hot*
*Change will be the essence of your life."*

*She dropped my hands and looked up at me. "Your destiny is not here, if you remain disaster will befall you." Well, it wasn't what I wanted to hear, but with the hairs on my arm standing up I knew it was time and not some ploy to get rid of me. It was this reason that I left New Orleans. And only by mistake on my part that I ended up going north along the same track I came. I had a stopover in Miridid, Mississippi as this is where my ride dropped me off. As luck had it, my next ride was a local and let me crash on the couch. The two meals were even more appreciated. He dropped me off at the exact spot on I-85 that he picked me up. Twenty minutes later I got a ride all the way to Atlanta.*

*No sooner was I dropped off, I began hitchhiking again and ten to fifteen minutes later Johnny picked me up. Johnny worked for a metal building company out of Zebulon, Georgia and was actually looking for someone to hire. I said sure and started at 8.50 an hour. As this was 1985, and not having any real expenses to speak of, this was actually really good money. I worked over the next few months with the company, crashing at Johnny's place first and later got my own place a few blocks away. As it turned out I ended up giving my job away to someone else who needed it much more and left. I purchased a motorcycle, though never transferred the title or plates into my name, and went west.*

*After a minor pause along the Mississippi River moving south along it until I hit a bridge, I continued on in a winding path that didn't actually have a specific direction until I turned on I-10 outside of Lake Charles, Louisiana. From there, I didn't stop except to eat, sleep get gas or use the bathroom. I should point out though that by day two of this my ass was nearly permanently numb, my walk was similar to a cowboy's who'd been in the saddle too long and I needed a break. That break was in Tucson, lasted a day where I relaxed by the pool, ate, did laundry and slept in a real bed. Considering that I had slept on the ground outside Midland, Texas the night before, the hotel was a joy. I got a late start the next day and didn't get any further than Yuma. Having seen three dead rattlesnakes between Tucson and Yuma, I decided to get another hotel room. I called a guy named Darryl in San Diego, telling him I'd be there the next day; again hung out at the pool, met some chick named Tammy and spent the next ten or twelve hours drinking and having sex. Tammy wanted to come with me. I said no and left.*

*Darryl had given me directions to his place in balboa Park, but he still had to come get me at the nearby McDonalds and let me follow him back. It was with Darryl and his girlfriend that I stayed that I stayed for three weeks and then left ..."*

As John implied earlier, Nature is not a simple walk in the park and nothing in this universe is as clear as it seems – swords are double-edged. John – the child born covered in a caul on the night of a New Moon under the auspices of the Magickal number 3 – would, indeed, find his Fate at the end of his winding Path. There would be the fire of the sun on the day he found his final fate. There would also be the water of a drowning and there would be the blood not of his birth but of another's death. There would be the steel of his knife, too. John would also add two to his one to make three for his final and decisive journey. He met a man named Mark who would become his blood brother and a girl, introduced to him by Mark, a girl desperate for love and companionship named Tracy. The three set off for their Fate.

# First Quarter of the Moon: The "Wyrd" Crime

*"In the absence of willpower the most complete collection of virtues and talents is wholly worthless."*
Aleister Crowley

*"Paganism is wholesome because it faces the facts of life."*
Aleister Crowley

*"The joy of life consists in the exercise of one's energies, continual growth, constant change, the enjoyment of every new experience. To stop means simply to die. The eternal mistake of mankind is to set up an attainable ideal."*
Aleister Crowley

By the time John literally set out on the last leg of his path, his feet were set on the soil of North Carolina in North America of the 20th century, but his Mind and Soul were set in the Old Ways of the Pagan, the Heroic and the Ancient. He kept a Book of Shadows by now which was the journal of his journeys, his adventures, his ceremonies and the spells he found particularly powerful. He armed himself with sharp blades (a large Bowie knife, a curved Ghurka knife and a short, sharp dagger) and was able to draw in the powers of the life-force around him, to draw it in and shape it to his will. John marked himself with two potent symbols on his left arm: a wolf beneath a crescent moon and the name Aragorn.

The wolf all at once symbolizes creation and destruction; it is the wild side of humanity; it stalks alone while hunting its prey. It is, much like John in the woods by his father's house, a pathfinder, forging its own way through the woods. John once wrote of a time when he realized the wolf was his symbol. He was wandering in Wyoming on his motorcycle, out where the roads are long, straight and desolate when he met the Spirit of the Wolf.

*"The red wolf is trying to make a comeback but they are smaller than the gray wolf most people think about when the word wolf is used. The gray wolf and timber wolf are basically the same things. I only ran into one wild wolf in my life. At least I think I ran into it. I was out in Wyoming and pulled off the road to camp. I was east of Jackson Hole, heading for Casper. I made a tarp into a lean-to. I built a fire. I had bought some buffalo jerky in Jackson Hole and was eating that and then smoked some thorn apple leaves. Then, I don't know if I had a hallucination or was in a trance or if it all really happened, but suddenly there was a wolf on the opposite side of the fire from me, looking at me. I had ½ bag of jerky left, so I tossed it over the fire to the wolf. It looked down, then back to me. I had pulled my knife out, a 10 inch blade made from pieces of coil spring just in*

*case it tried to come at me. Unfortunately, I had been up for 36 hours and was dead on my feet. Even so I managed to keep awake for a while as this wolf was out there looking at me. But sleep took me away. I woke up with a start, thinking I had just nodded off for a moment. Maybe I knew I had slept for the rest of the night. A March snow was still there on the ground, part of the tarp was being used as a ground cover. The fire was out, tendrils of smoke rising from it. Cold and scared by the fact I had fallen asleep with a wolf looking at me, I got up and looked about for it. It was then I'd noticed the jerky was gone, bag and all, but there was no tracks of the wolf. Thinking I had been tripping, I looked into the burned out coals for the bag of jerky. Wasn't there, wasn't in my pockets or my saddlebags either. I broke camp and got out of there. At a truck stop I got brunch and filled up my tank. I kept thinking about that wolf. Real or imagined. If a real wolf, where did the tracks go? If an illusion, where did the jerky go? Never have worked it out. Yes, I realized that if it was real I'd be damn lucky to be alive."*

This was another experience in Nature that "marked" John, just as his trade with Herne had. From that moment on, he realized he had as much Wolf Spirit as any.

Yet John had always had an affinity for the Wolf and was at times possessed by the Spirit, taken away and then returned – even days later – with no knowledge of what he had been doing, where he had been or why there was a void in his consciousness. Friends also noted that he would suddenly "zone out," become despondent and even mimic the mannerisms of the Wolf.

*"... looking back now I think the Wolf has always been with me and within me. Exactly when this happened, the Wolf and I becoming one – or more like Two Inhabiting One Body – I couldn't say. I do know that I began to sense a Wolfish part of me and give it a name when I was around 17 years old. This is when I began to use the name Lupus to refer to myself. This later became DeCanis Lupus Verispelles, which is Latin. Why I used that language is that most people don't speak it and the star lupus is next to the star group that makes up the scales of Libra, my birth sign. Perhaps in this there has always been a connection to the Wolf, born to it. Yet it was more a feeling than a knowing. Knowing would come later. Perhaps this is the case with all "Lycanthropes," being born to it. As far as I know, I do not physically become a wolf, though I have often dreamt of being a Wolf, hunting, playing, generally being a wolf. However, there are times of extreme stress when I slip mentally and I have no recollection of events. Sometimes these periods are short, only a handful of minutes. Other times, hours pass before I am aware of being myself or remember what is going on. The longest period of this not-being-conscious of what is going on has been three days. I went to work, though I hardly spoke to anyone. I showed up at work*

*wondering why no one was at the job site. It was a Saturday. The last memory I could bring forth was getting off work on Tuesday and fixing a chicken pot pie to eat. After that, nothing. Even today I will become aware of gaps in my memory. As before, I can tell there is a "last time". Watching the TV and then realize I missed sections of the story, having conversations here with someone and then not having it. I call down to the person I was having the conversation with and they say I just "zoned out." Many people have told me I get this look in my eyes; some say I've actually growled at them."*

Aragorn, John's other tattoo, was a literary symbol for him, though no less powerful. The name comes from the mythology of J.R.R. Tolkien. Also known as Strider, Aragorn was in some ways John's literary alter ego: a dispossessed soul of mysterious, ancient origins who strived to attain greatness in the world. Aragorn's father was killed in a battle with Orcs, while John had killed off any sense of emotional attachment he had for his father after he had traveled many miles to see him, only to be told badly he had messed things up. Not only did John's father die that day, but so did any sense of attachment to others. Aragorn, fatherless as was John, was also reared in foster situations in a place called Rivendell. By all accounts, John had become a tall, strong physical creature who was generally quiet and tinged by sadness, yet had outbursts of levity; so Aragorn was described as well. Both Aragorn and John were sworn by their mothers to keep their lineage a secret lest the society around them track them down and kill them. Most importantly, John, since the day he was marked by Herne, had set out to reassemble the pieces of his legacy, to weave together the strands of his heritage into one magical cord, a past that had been hinted to him by his mother and sisters and castigated by his father.

John knew the Ogham, the runes and the old languages. He had studied them and made notes in his Book of Shadows. John knew that this Old World that had enveloped him was one driven by this idea of the Wyrd. Words in the Old Days were not what they are now. Their meanings were elusive, flexible and even personal. A word was Magickal and one had to master them, not just let them fall out one's mouth. When John's father had lied to him, misusing his words, that was an evil spell and John saw no life in his father after that day. Wyrd eventually became codified as "weird" or "difficult to understand," but that is the most superficial of its meanings. Of course when one looks into the crystal ball of one's future, things may seem hard to understand, and oracles can sometimes be riddles and just as confusing. Not all our heroes know where they are headed all the time. They know only that they are on a path and are heading somewhere – and that touches on the oldest and truest meaning of the word: "to come to pass" or "becoming." So John was becoming what he was supposed to be.

There were three – that magical number again – when John set out on his final journey, the one that would bring him to the still point of his life, the hub of the wheel if you will. Mark was his sworn friend and one in whom John had all placed his confidence. Nothing, John had sworn with blood on his palm oozing from a cut from his blade, will come between us. Mark cut his palm and they put their palms together and held tight. They were joined by blood now – blood calls to blood. Mark had also adorned himself with the symbols by which he wanted to be recognized. There was an unfinished Grim Reaper on his back; a spear and a shield indicating that he prepared for battle; Celtic knot-work and tribal imagery twisting along his flesh; a Celtic dog baying beneath a crescent moon; a dragon and a nude lady; a nude Devil's daughter and a rendering of the Greek God of Frenzy and Intoxication, the God who was torn apart by his own followers, Bacchus. All of these symbols from the Old Days come together to paint a collage of a wild Soul bent on pleasure, best expressed by the figure of Bacchus, the God of Wine. Bacchus was the outsider god who was followed by a throng of female revelers and bearded satyrs, known for their sexual potency; his female followers, the maenads, would feed the dead through blood sacrifices made in His honor; he was the communicator between the dead and the living.

Tracy joined the blood brothers, mostly because she had the car and some money. Mark had introduced John to Tracy; Mark had known her and called her "easy." The girl was led easily because she wanted to have a boyfriend and eventually a family; she wanted to grow up and get away from her mother. John said the only way to move on to the next stage of her life was to move out, see the world – head South with us, he suggested. So, the three of them drove south in Tracy's car toward the Oldest City in America, Saint Augustine.

There were signs of bad fortune in South Carolina, signals that things were taking a bad turn and that this Path John was traveling would reveal his Fate, yet may not be the stuff of fairy tales. There is an old Latin proverb that says "fate leads those who are willing and drags those who are not," so the three were dragged along as things started to go badly. The gear tied to the back of the car fell off; John hadn't tied it tightly enough. Tracy complained. John and Tracy bickered the whole way. She was ruining the journey, distracting him from his destiny. By the time the three pulled over for gas somewhere in South Carolina, the mood was dour. As Mark tightened up the ropes holding down the gear on the back of the car, John came out of the gas station convenience store and said he wanted to get rid of Tracy. He had enough of her nonsense, her bickering. Thinking little of it, Mark kept at his work. The three got back in the car with a thick animus in the air as they headed farther south.

The three arrived in Saint Augustine, a city founded by the Spanish during the quest for the mystical Fountain of Youth. For years, Old World Europeans, the Spanish especially, had heard wild tales from the Indians about these springs that shot up from the earth and the pools of healing waters they supplied. These waters held Magick; they healed the sick; they prolonged life. Supposedly, there are such springs in Saint Augustine. The ancient Indians worshiped in the area, building huge cairns or mounds where massive energy is accumulated. And just as John believed that artifacts handed down through the generations in a family hold the energy of that heritage, so did this city seem to hold its energy and spirit. In the Old Fort, spirits of the imprisoned in the dungeon moan and wail; Spanish soldiers still mark their watch dutifully. The lighthouse is still manned by a loyal ghost who, according to some, still shines a light for wayward seafarers. Even the playgrounds are haunted by three little girls who fell out a wheelbarrow during a construction accident; they laugh and frolic on the swings. Some even believe a ley line runs north-south through the city and another runs east-west from Saint Augustine, connecting to other powerful centers of energy such as New Orleans. That would make the place where the three stopped a nodal point, a pinpoint of the map of the earth where serious power gathers, swirling like the ingredients in an alchemists cauldron, brewing the future fates of those who tread on those aged cobblestones. It is also the seat of Saint John's County, all of its tributaries being fed by the Saint John's River, an ancient, snaking body of water dotted by Indian remnants of worship.

It was the summer solstice when they arrived, also known as the Feast of Saint John for Christians, another co-opted Sabbath according to John. On the other end of the ley line that runs through Saint Augustine, in New Orleans, the Crescent City known for "conjure men," Voudoun, zombies, potions and magical powders, they celebrate Saint John's Eve, one of the most important holidays on the Voodoun calendar. By the time the three had arrived, settled into their hotel room, and John made up his mind to get rid of Tracy, the Eve of St, John ceremony was under way. Throngs of Voodoun worshipers gather by a place called St. John Bayou. A big altar is erected on the ground, covered with food for the Gods and snakes that writhe over the God's Feast. The Queen climbs atop the altar and begins to gyrate, to shake and to dance until the Spirits possess her. Then, at just the right moment, she puts a picture of Saint John on the ground; the ceremony has begun. All the worshipers then go to the altar and knock on it once, twice and three times for the Trinity of faith, hope and charity. Everyone engages in a Creole dance, two women for one man, all in threes, the men switching off between women as he dances. The crowd of trios works itself to fever pitch, grinding hips against each other, drinking rum and beer, and after a while the Queen signals and everyone runs mad into the bayou.

For Pagans such as John, it was the time of Litha, which came from the Midsummer Ceremonies of the Old Days. It was a celebration of the sun at its solstice ("sol"= sun and "stice" = still) when the sun was still in its rotation for a spell and burned in the sky, heading southward again. This was a favorite time of the year for John, starting with the fertility rites of May Day and running into the summer solstice.

*"Well Beltane has always been a favorite of mine. The imagery of sex is huge. The maypole with its red and white ribbons is a major fertility symbol; a poll is the phallic symbol, the white is the man the red is the symbol of the woman. Dancers take up the ribbons according to gender. Males of sexual maturity, but not married, take up the white, and females of sexual maturity, but also not married, take up the red, the numbers being equal. The females go clockwise and male counterclockwise; then out until the ribbons are too short, having been weaved about the poll. The male and female facing each other are paired for the day at the end of the maypole dance. Then they rush off into the forest to gather greens and more times than not "green wood" marriages happen. In the olden times, the age of these youths averaged between 14 and 20, but in smaller villages the age was technically open to anyone who was able to procreate and was not married. Fact is, Beltane was the traditional day of getting married, usually under a Hawthorne tree. It took place among the crops at night. There also is an Irish tradition for older ones to have sex in the fields. It is said that dew collected on the morning of May 1 would make them powerful or keep them looking young. Personally, I missed the idea of the ancient pagans where people would dash out into the woods, and relieved of the duty of spouses, have sex with whoever was willing. But there is no guilt, just a pleasure and experience of the new. It was the children born on or about this time who are considered special having been conceived on or around Beltane. Of course in today's social climate of paternity tests and such, they would all end up on Maury or on Jerry Springer. Summer festivals can be just as fun, but in large gatherings of pagan's like they have in Bloomington, Indiana for summer solstice. Yes, there are some that are there, waving around their plastic magic wands, while prancing about like a court jester on acid; but you just have to overlook the crap and the tricks."*

The old Pagans, the Druids, used to light massive bonfires in the dark night; they knew that evil spirits roamed free when the sun headed southward again. It was a very dangerous time if not taken and treated properly. Were those the evil spirits that climbed into John and animated him, filling him with hatred for Tracy?

When they arrived, the moon was in the first quarter heading toward the height of its powers – a full moon – on the 26th. They arrived on 6/20/1991, just before the celebrations of the solstice were to get under way. It was a 1 day:

$$6+2+0+1+9+9+1=28$$
$$2+8=10$$
$$1+0=1$$

A day ruled by the number one is a day that is ruled by the Sun, the center of the universe, that which gives life with its warmth and light; it creates illumination. It signals creation, new beginnings, strength. Some call it the God Number because 1 cannot be divided without multiplying, sometimes infinitely: $1/3=.333333$ ad infinitum. It is everything to which we aspire: 6 is the number of imperfect man, or man who is becoming something through his Wyrd life path, and when 1 is added, he becomes a 7, the imperfect man plus the creative spirit, or perfection. But just as light illuminates, it casts shadows, and this can spill over into destruction, a beginning can be an ending and the spiritual perfection that the 1 lends may not be the beginning of a new Path but the end of one that one has been traveling. Thus, the three travelers drove head on into a cosmic maelstrom of powerful numbers, astrological signs and portents and into one of the most powerful areas in North America.

None the less, John, Mark and Tracy got a hotel room where they decided to stay until they found jobs. They bickered again. Mark and John went out to look for jobs and a place in an old boarding house, one drenched in the history of the city. John told the landlord that it would only be Mark and John. Mark asked John where Tracy would be staying. John said he was going to kill her.

On June 25th, Tracy talked to her mother. That would be the last time that she would speak with her mother – or anyone. Litha had ended; the St. John ceremonies were over; the sun was heading southward and the evil spirits had been unleashed. Those malicious demons poked at the rage Herne had marked John with early on in his life, like stoking the Fires of Hell. John couldn't wait any more, so he and Mark invited Tracy to a party out in the woods. Knowing that her fate was intertwined with these two, and all of her hopes of having a boyfriend and any sort of family, she followed.

They had all been drinking beer. The night was dark and the moon was almost full when they left; all the sunlight was gone and sheets of rain fell hard on the ground, welling up into deep puddles. John drove through the rainy darkness looking for a bridge that crossed over one of the tributaries of the Saint John River. His plan was to feed her corpse to the alligators when he was done. John found one, drove down the access road in the soggy earth. The three of them got out and followed a trail into the woods, Tracy in the rear of the two men. They could not find the path that led to the water. Mark got tired of slogging through the water which at times was up to their shins; he turned back and headed for the car. Mark heard a scream; he turned around and headed towards John in the rain. According to police reports, this is what Mark saw:

"John had Tracy [sic] from behind and was like backing up, keeping her feet off the ground, and she was struggling and still screaming. And then I saw his hand come up, and I saw the knife in his hand, and I saw him… I saw him stab her at least one time. I don't know how many other times… at least once. And then he threw her on the ground in the middle of the clearing and sat on her back, pretty much looked at her, and then he saw she was still alive. And the water was, you know, pretty deep; so he held her head under water till she quit breathing. Then he handed me the knife, and I washed the blood off it. And then she jerked like, you know, like-like a gasp or something, and I thought she was still alive… And he put her head under water again and, you know, made sure. Then he told me to stab her. She was already dead, but he told me to stab her. So I did. And I washed it off and gave the knife back to him."

Mark then hacked at Tracy's neck with a second knife. John tried to dig a hole to bury the body (they were too far from the water to let the alligators take care of her) but there were too many roots. They went through her pockets and took some money and a knife. Then they went back to the hotel to wash away the blood that marked what turned out to be the most vicious, most brutal and most crucial point in John's life, the baby born in a caul on a 3 Day, a Sunday 25 years earlier (2+5=7). He committed this act on 6/25/1991, a day with double the power of his birth day:

$$6+2+5+1+9+9+1= 33$$
$$3+3=6$$
$$6$$

He was, according to the numbers, at the moment of the act which shaped his Path and his life on this plane for ever more, born again (3 plus another 3) but in the end, marked by the number of Man, imperfect, foolish, impulsive Man, who acts greedily, lustfully, angrily and with great destruction all too often.

It was not until after midnight – with the visions of the blood, rain, mud and screaming still in his head – that the blood had been washed away. He was in new, dry clothes. His knives were cleaned and put away – all three of them. A full moon hung in the opaque blackness of the sky outside the window of his boarding house room in the oldest city in America, ghosts swirling through the air with the evil spirits unleashed with the recession of the sun. The moon had gained all its power; so had John. He felt it in him, but he also felt that in this moment, there was an end and a stillness like that which the sun had felt days before, revolving on its own axis for just a moment before it headed south to die its death in winter. It was 6/26/1991:

$$6+2+6+1+9+9+1=34$$
$$3+4=7$$
$$7$$

Christians believe that the number six is the number of man-incomplete – struggling, laboring, wanting the completion of God, whose day is the 7th. The serpent was created on the 6th day. Other schools of thought believe it is the number of decisions that need to be made, crucial decisions. The sixth commandment rails against the sin of murder, but John did not believe in commandments or sins. He believed in the exertion of the Will, the Life Force, of that Wyrd Path we travel and hopefully find Enlightenment at the end of. Looking from the outside in, it may seem odd that as he stood there in that old boarding house room, just having taken a life for little more than 150 dollars and a knife in terms of material possessions John knew that he had gained much more than those few bucks, those trinkets. He was 6 and then that one piece was added, that impervious God Number that crowns the seeker after a long journey and brings him to that point of rest, of stillness and of an uneasy peace.

Christians celebrate the birth of Christ as their savior on December 25th, during the darkest time of the year, when the light slowly returns until it is Spring again and life is returned to nature. Satanists, however, place the birth of Satan at just after midnight on June 25th, right after the birth of the first prophet, Saint John and his celebration of Light and the longest day of the year. Edmond Lautreamont even went so far as to prophesy the birth of the Anti-Christ on the 25th of June in 1966 (666), the same year John was born in a caul. And, here was John born again in the light of the longest day and in the darkness of the Anti-Christ himself. He was, according to his Pagan beliefs in his heart and soul and all that he had vowed and sealed in blood, alive – perhaps more vital and powerful than ever. Yet, according to the Christian/Biblical laws of the land that surrounded him, he was anathema, anti-Christian and had to be killed for his "sin."

# Persecution

*"The supreme satisfaction is to be able to despise one's neighbor and this fact goes far to account for religious intolerance. It is evidently consoling to reflect that the people next door are headed for hell."*
Aleister Crowley

*"The virtue of paganism was strength; the virtue of Christianity is obedience."*
Augustus Hare

1966, the year of John's biological birth, was a year that marked the beginning of a new era of occult powers and concentration. According to Lautreamont, Satan was born again in a 33-year cycle. This was also the year that Anton Lavey started The Church of Satan, which drew its name from the Christian idea of Satan, and claims that every individual can be his or her own god and is responsible for his or her own destiny. Lavey chose one of the most important occult holidays, in one of the most numerologically important years in the occult world, to launch his church, Walpurgis Night, April 30, 1966. (4+3+0+1+9+6+6=29. 2+9=11. 11 is a double 1 or God Number; God to the second power.) 3 years later, Lavey published his Satanic Bible, which purported a new ideology, contrary to Christianity that embraced the carnal, the sexual, the vital and things that seemed, at least to him and his followers, essentially true and without hypocrisy:

The Nine Satanic Statements
1. Satan represents indulgence instead of abstinence.
2. Satan represents vital existence instead of spiritual pipe dreams.
3. Satan represents undefiled wisdom instead of hypocritical self-deceit.
4. Satan represents kindness to those who deserve it instead of love wasted on ingrates.
5. Satan represents vengeance instead of turning the other cheek.
6. Satan represents responsibility to the responsible instead of concern for psychic vampires.
7. Satan represents man as just another animal, sometimes better, more often worse than those that walk on all-fours, who, because of his "divine spiritual and intellectual development", has become the most vicious animal of all.
8. Satan represents all of the so-called sins, as they all lead to physical, mental, or emotional gratification.
9. Satan has been the best friend the Church has ever had, as He has kept it in business all these years.

The Nine Satanic Sins
1. Stupidity
2. Pretentiousness
3. Solipsism
4. Self-deceit
5. Herd Conformity
6. Lack of Perspective
7. Forgetfulness of Past Orthodoxies
8. Counterproductive Pride
9. Lack of Aesthetics

The Eleven Satanic Rules of the Earth
1. Do not give opinions or advice unless you are asked.
2. Do not tell your troubles to others unless you are sure they want to hear them.
3. When in another's lair, show them respect or else do not go there.
4. If a guest in your lair annoys you, treat them cruelly and without mercy.
5. Do not make sexual advances unless you are given the mating signal.
6. Do not take that which does not belong to you unless it is a burden to the other person and they cry out to be relieved.
7. Acknowledge the power of magic if you have employed it successfully to obtain your desires. If you deny the power of magic after having called upon it with success, you will lose all you have obtained.
8. Do not complain about anything to which you need not subject yourself.
9. Do not harm little children.
10. Do not kill non-human animals unless you are attacked or for your food.
11. When walking in open territory, bother no one. If someone bothers you, ask them to stop. If they don't stop, destroy them.

Though John claimed to be an Older, perhaps "truer", version of the Pagan-occultists than Lavey, who was seen rubbing elbows with Hollywood types and was involved in the demise of Jayne Mansfield, the precepts that Lavey laid out in his version of the Bible seem to equal many of John's basic beliefs. Sensuality and sexuality were prized, as long as it did not infringe on someone else's happiness; the property of others was to be respected; magical powers had to be respected and revered; others, including animals were not to be killed, unless they impinged on your life. Murder was only a sin if it was not justified. The real sins had to do with too much pride in one's self and stupidity – being part of the "herd." Of course, a Christian seeing these precepts would deem them evil, contrary to the laws of the Bible and those that were scrawled in stone and supposedly handed to Moses by God himself.

Unfortunately for John, he knew he was to be judged in a court that rested upon the foundation of Christian morals and not those of his beliefs if he were to be caught by the police. John was newly reborn nonetheless, baptized in blood just as on the day he was born in 1966. Still, John and Mark – now only two that the trio had been shattered – knew that staying in the haunted city of Saint Augustine was not a good idea. The original idea was to feed Tracy's body to the alligators that prowled the shallow tributary waters of the Saint John River, but the path had been flooded, washed away and lost. Thus, the butchered body remained somewhere out there underneath that bridge off that access road. When the flood waters receded the body would dry up somewhere, on a hammock or on the shore where some fisherman would stumble upon it. Mark suggested heading to the other coast, along the Gulf of Mexico, and heading south again. John had different ideas. John wanted to follow his path, since now it had been taken to new heights. A key component of John's philosophy, and that of Occultists such as Aleister Crowley, for instance, was the exertion of the individual will upon the world to create a reality. Of course, this was anti-Christian. In Christianity, one was supposed to submit the will-force to one God in Heaven, as a slave submits to a master. John, however, could never reconcile his mind or his actions to this idea of submission. He was a creature of Nature, and, just as seeds and leaves settle on the wind and fall here or there, so would John, but he needed Nature around him in order to connect with the physical earth, create his Magick and his world. He and Mark ended up in Pinellas County, Florida, a place that by 1991 was in a seeming race to cover every piece of nature except for the tourist-trap beaches. There were strip malls, traffic, fumes, trailer parks, renovated bungalows, fast-food chains, banks and commerce – everything but nature. Everyone, according to John, seemed to be trying to get somewhere but was getting nowhere; this was the crux of Modern Society that John may have hated the most. There was a synthetic feel to this place for him and a bad energy permeated the whole scene:

*"As for what I thought of the Pinellas County, too many towns packed together and not enough country area. Too many run down and poor neighborhoods. A distinct uneasy/undertone running through the place. Like everyone is too busy to be busy yet not really getting ahead. The beaches are more relaxed, though that may be because of the tourists there. True there are neighborhoods that are islands of peace and prosperity or at least a façade of it but the rest is jumpy, unsettled, nervous energy. Mind you this was my impression in 1991. I honestly did not want to settle there. I need open land and forests. This was my co-defendant's idea, not mine. I wanted to go north and west, far west and north, someplace with four actual seasons and snow. But I allowed him to talk me into it, said he had jobs lined up for us in Naples. They fell through. Should have left right then."*

In fact, Pinellas County was not just full of negative energy and lacked open spaces for worship, but, perhaps because of this, it was bereft of Pagan worshipers:

*"The number of covens that were public are pretty much zero; the majority of pagans then and now are solitary or small family groups. Organized covens existed, but they were usually closed circles that are hard to join, harder to find. Back then occult stores were contact places. But even so there were bulletin board systems; today they're called web sites, that a few Pagans would make contact with each other. I know there is a place in Zephyrhills where a group meets. Some of the members are from Tampa. I had heard of the group in Sarasota, but never met anyone from there. However, my guess would be there were perhaps 500 Pagans in the St. Pete area. I guess that at least that many are in Tampa. But that is just a guess. The ones I met were mixture of young and old, professional and nonprofessional, a few with kids younger siblings etc., and almost all were not in a coven, beyond that of a family unit. I'd say that the majority were Wiccan; some were wannabes and non-prescribed to the form of Old World Paganism that I do. No blood oaths, not anything I consider as fully embracing witchcraft. Though one woman came close. She worked for [a communications firm] in data entry I think, single mother of one daughter age five at the time living with her father. We traded books, almost had a relationship, but didn't go that far. Not that I wasn't willing or she wasn't. It just didn't get that far. I wasn't there long enough to really get tight with people there."*

In the end, Pinellas was not the open, natural space full of devoted Pagans John was looking for or cared for. It was, in fact, the antithesis of everything he wanted.

As it was, John ended up living in one of the oldest, most congested parts of Pinellas County, off of one of the busiest roads in the county, one that slows to a crawl when the business-people, who are "busy getting nowhere", try to hurry home. He worked for a printing firm and lived in a shed behind a house where he kicked in for bills and paid the rent once in a while. This was supposed to be a temporary stop-over. Mark and John never got to Naples, however.

Mark took off in Tracy's car and was about to head north without John. On 11/11/1991, two hunters went down into the Valino salt marshes to go hunting. They found a partially decomposed body that had been decapitated. It was scantily hidden beneath some brush and some sticks. The hunters reported the body to police who later identified it as Tracy. Mark was then caught driving Tracy's car in Pinellas and was arrested when police found a knife and brass knuckles in his possession. He confessed that the weapons were his, was arrested and said Tracy had sold the car to him and John for two hundred dollars; John had the bill of sale. John was still in Pinellas County and was quickly found and arrested only 6 days later on a Saturday, the 6th day of the week.

On 9-19-1991 (9+1+9+1+9+9+1=39  3+9=12  1+2= 3) Mark was pulled over in Pinellas County while driving the car registered to Tracy, who at the time was missing. Mark had violated his parole in North Carolina, so he was arrested and North Carolina was contacted. When contacted John said the same thing as Mark, yet police kept on investigating and found out John was living at 8557 92nd (8+5+5+7+9+2=39  3+6= 9  9= 3x3) Terrace North in a town called Seminole in a small shack out behind the house. Detectives arrived and asked John to come with them to the sheriff's department for questioning. He went without incident and without knowing that two days prior an arrest warrant had been issued for him in Saint John's County on 11-17-1991 (1+1+1+7+1+9+9+1= 30  3+0= 3).

Years later, John still rails at the validity of his arrest and the circumstances of his interrogation:

A sequence of events in the case of John -- and how he is likely to be killed due to a faulty justice system and appeals procedure.

On November 17th, 1991 defendant was picked up by police at his residence in Pinellas County, Florida for what he was told was routine questioning. This was in fact a lie as an arrest warrant had already been issued. Hence, defendant, once in custody was not free to leave, but was not informed of his status.

Defendant was under the influence of LSD at the time of questioning. When he was processed into the Pinellas County Jail the on-duty nurse was so concerned for the health – racing heart and high blood pressure along with elevated temperature – of the defendant that she took three vials of blood and put him into a medical observation cell.

At first appearance, in front of the judge via video/closed circuit television, the judge denied counsel (attorney) to defendant. That being a constitutional safeguard given to all people charged with any crime. Later, when defendant requested the tape the attorney who was later appointed went to Pinellas County where the tape was "accidentally" erased while trying to copy it. But only the part where defendant was denied an attorney. Defendant instructed attorney to obtain paperwork, or lack of paperwork, from the public Defender's office in Pinellas County to show no attorney had been appointed to deal with defendant's case. The trial attorney did not do this.

While being held in Pinellas County Jail without council, but after first appearance when he was supposed to be afforded representation, the police/sheriff deputies took defendant out of the jail where he was again interrogated without representation present (how could there be when none was appointed, actually denied defendant council?) where so-called written statement was obtained. Though the handwriting of the statement is not the same of the defendant.

No Medical Records or blood sample taken from defendant could be found according to trial attorney. The only conclusion for this is that evidence was destroyed. Court records of the proceeding at first appearance were also destroyed in the presence of trial attorney.

John, seemingly not in complete control of his faculties, signed Consent to Search Waiver which gave the detectives the complete authority to check the shack that he had fashioned into his hermit's hut in the middle of a semi-urban jungle. Three (3) detectives went back to 8557 92nd Terrace North to search for knives. When they arrived at the hut, the same guys were sitting at John's table. Two detectives went in and searched with the "subjects present," except for John who was still locked away. Among John's mundane items – like the Colt Paperback series, reams of paper, New Age catalogs, cassette tapes and clothing – the detectives found everything John needed to escape Westward and disappear into the wilds where the earth would always be on his feet and the sun – or rain – would always be on his head, and, as the Irish say, the wind would always be at his back. John had military survival guides and survival gear, even survivalist magazines, as well as a Marines cold weather survival guide. There were bags full of crude, homemade incense. More bags filled with tallow-dipped candles and dozens of candle holders, no doubt to form his altars in the Western woods. There were knives and bullets. Double-sided knives, a buck knife, all together 7 knives were found. Pads were filled with notes on plants, dried herbs and how to crush and combine them to heal wounds and cure disease. Chisels and darts lay about. There were two Books of Shadows. Three (3) plastic jars were found as well. Two had the name DeLupus written on them; one was empty and another was filled with white powder. The third had "poison" written on it with a skull and crossbones scrawled on a paper label. All of this and more was entered into evidence, but they, quite frankly, did not know what to make of most of it. It was as if they had walked into a portal and were quarked back hundreds of years into the hut of some Celtic shaman on a Scottish heath, leaving them as dumbfounded as a Roman centurion poking through the charms and talismans of an Old Pagan Holy Man.

65

Pythagoras believed that numbers dictated everything in the universe, every movement, every spasm of the cosmic or what we might call the Divine. Numbers were the values of motion, the geometry of our experience. That being the case, John's life was figured by this sacred number 3, some ethereal algebra destined him to find his way south to Saint Augustine and then to those salt marshes as the Moon waxed above him. Then, as ironic and absurd as the ending of his Path seems, he was destined to be judged by twelve jurors and one judge (13) and sent to Death Row.

The laws of this country are still basically the same laws that came from the Christian Bible, that book that John despised his whole life, and the Christian Church, that entity he reviled just as much, for it was the opposite of everything he had sought while on his path; it was something that had tracked, hunted and persecuted his Pagan people for centuries, chasing them from one continent to the next and shedding their blood. And here was John, in 21st century America, the Land of the Free, the home of religious freedom, being persecuted by laws that were etched in stone over 2000 years ago. In Exodus 21:12-14, the ancient Biblical law states:

"12Anyone who strikes a man and kills him shall surely be put to death. 13However, if he does not do it intentionally, but God lets it happen, he is to flee to a place I will designate. 14But if a man schemes and kills another man deliberately, take him away from my altar and put him to death."

The jury of twelve and the judge, making 13, heard the gruesome details of what had happened to Tracy in the salt marshes that night. They had heard from Mark how John had been the ringleader and how he had forced Mark to hack at Tracy's body that rainy night – that Mark was just a follower. Then, they heard from doctors who had interviewed John and decided he was a smart enough guy but that he was "anti-social" and that caused him not to see the validity of social laws, which were really just Biblical laws. The courtroom was filled with testimony from social workers who recounted the stories of how John was fascinated with knives and combat and that they believed he needed more help than they could give him, but they did not know that his Soul had been marked by the fierce spirit of an ancient hunter who patrolled the heart of England, Herne. The jury was told it happened in Saint Augustine, but no one mentioned that there were ghosts all through that town; no one said that at the solstice evil spirits roam free, unfettered by the veil that normally protects our world from them. John's soul could have been possessed at that time. No one looked at the numbers of the day. They only saw the surface of things and disregarded that he was raised in a house with a coffee-table that turned into an altar, a soup pot that made a good cauldron and a chopping board that hid a pentagram. When his mother was interviewed, they did not see she was a Celtic-Blackfoot Indian hedge witch; no, they saw a lady who had been a drunk and who fought constantly with the father; they saw a young man with Parental Alienation Syndrome. No one knew he cast spells and vowed his blood to the Gods of Old. John believed the whole trial had been a complete sham, another Old world persecution of an Outsider and that the attempt to understand what had truly had happened in those salt marshes on that rainy night was half-hearted at beast:

At the mid-point before the start of the trial, trial attorney was notified that he was also representing a key witness in the case, one Hobart Harison, who was the state's key witness in the trial of Mark, also charged in the case but tried separately. Defendant told attorney to call defense witnesses to rebut and counter the credibility of Mark's testimony at trial. Trial attorney refused to call the witnesses saying later at an evidentiary hearing later in December 1999 that he felt Harison would have been hostile and thus make a poor witness. (In this the reasonable thing to do for an attorney is to resign from the case so that other attorneys might be appointed to represent Defendant.) The trial attorney said it was trial strategy not to call these witnesses but there was no reasonable strategy in this decision. The credibility of witnesses cannot be called into question either as the State felt at the earlier trial that they were very credible.

*"My trial was a farce. My trial attorneys during the "guilt phase" failed to redirect, rebut testimony or call potential witnesses to refute testimony given by State's witnesses. During the penalty phase (after jury conviction) the entire investigation and strategy of the proceeding was given over to a non-attorney. This violates US Supreme Court ruling of Wiggins, specifically that the only ineffective council claims that could be raised in direct appeal were those contained and reviewable through the record. That any other IAC claims are to be raised on the 3.850 Collateral Appeal after the direct appeal.*

*All well and good until I get to the Federal level where I was procedurally barred from making any IAC claims because the issues were not brought up in direct appeal proceedings. In essence, due to the ineptitude of my Direct appeal attorney in either understanding the procedures of the direct appeals and Federal Rules and Procedures of the Court or the Public Defender intentionally misled me and sabotaged my Federal Appeals early on. The third option is that there are discrepancies between state and federal courts which are causing me and many others from fully pursuing the avenues of the appeals process. In truth, causing defaults of it self, merely by existing.*

*There are grounds to overturn this case, either in part or totally reversing this case under ruling by the US Supreme Court. Ruling that lower courts have chosen to intentionally ignore knowing that their rulings will cause them any judicial sanctions. In essence, usurping the authority of the High Court with impunity."*

This also does not even begin to consider the fact that the defendant is unable to recall facts of the night in which the crime was committed. The defendant was intoxicated that night coupled with the long standing "mental illness" reaching back into childhood where at two periods he was committed to mental institutions for treatment. There was the fact that there were, through various means, even that of the depositions of Abshire to law enforcement. Glossed over by the judicial rulings by the court and not even given an exacting investigation.

During December 1991 Evidentiary Hearing, one doctor made comments to this effect, that the examinations given to evaluate the defendant were severely deficient and alluded that had further test been performed the results would have been much different. It should also be noted here that the doctor that carried out the examination is also a professional witness for the State of Florida who is always willing to accommodate the state to retain his income. A review of his diagnosis over the years will render this opinion out to be truthful for he has probably never rendered a diagnosis which had gone contrary to the state's intent.

However, this is an opinion as I have never been able to review his material.

There was another trial attorney assigned to the case. An attorney who, if he ever won a trial in a First Degree Murder Case I would have to uncover it. Hence, the best choice in the state's opinion, to represent clients facing such charges for he is seen as an asset to the state. The conviction the state has gotten while he defended are the least likely to be overturned as he was an expert in dotting his "I"'s and crossing his "t"'s where the procedures are concerned yet not really giving his clients the best defense he could.

As for appeals process... there have been between 10 to 14 attorneys who have had their hands in it. This constant parade of varying counsel has only served to undermine the quality of work.

So, they, in their limited world view, opted for the most obvious and typical answer a 21st century jury could and they followed the advice of that 2000-plus year old tome, the Bible: "'If anyone takes the life of a human being, he must be put to death." (Leviticus 24:17) To them, it was all black and white, good versus evil.

To John, he was cast into a place that was un-natural, inorganic; a place that lacked humanity. As one Death Row inmate in the same prison put it. "Have I ever explained to you how this building is? There are six wings and two stories. A run has 14 cells. A floor has 28 cells. Front of the cell is bars. Then there if the hallway 5' wide, then another wall. The there is a 3' wide hallway (called Catwalk), and then the outside wall that concrete. That wall has windows in it but the way they are made they don't let much air in when the exhaust fans don't work. There is no A/C. The only A/C is in the guard's station and visiting room. In the back of each cell there is 20'' by 20'' exhaust vent. Back side of this run is the same. There is a 3' wide pipe ally between the cells. And is where the exhaust fans are at. There are 7 big exhaust fans on the top of each wing. The problem is that only two of them are working. Those two pull most of the air through the five that not working and nothing through the cells. Therefore it gets hotter than fish grease in those cells during the day. I'm told this wing is hotter because the others don't have as many fans not working. Plus this wing points NE so it has sun on it most of the day."

Another Death Row inmate on another wing describes the same monotonous routine, the isolation and the basic hunger. "At the Death Row facility where I am being housed, inmates are confined to one-man cells 24 hours a day. That is, all day long every day, unless the inmate is summoned by prison officials, the medical department, goes to a shower cell, recreation, or if lucky occasionally receives a visit from a family member or friend. Each cell is a 6'X9' cubical comprised of three solid concrete walls and the traditional steel bar grill serving as the front wall which provides an open view of the cell to all passers-by. Accommodations in each cell, unless it is a security cell, include: a steel bunk coupled with a thin cotton mat, a wall mounted steel table which is too high to use, a locker box for storage, sink, toilet, and a ceiling mounted fluorescent light. The only people one can see are guards making rounds. There is no carpet on the floors, or central heat and air conditioning. During the winter the cellblocks can be unbearably cold; during the summer, unbearably hot and humid.

Meals are delivered to the inmate in his cell. Each inmate is fed three times a day. Two hot meals which are always cold and one cold meal. It is a meager diet hardly sufficient to satiate the average adult appetite. Prisoners that enjoy the financial support of family members and friends can counterbalance the poor diet with canteen items such as sandwiches, chips, candy bars, etc. Not uncommonly, the indigent prisoners face long hungry nights, as it is approximately fourteen hours in between the last evening meal and breakfast the next morning.

Day to day activities generally include: talking, playing chess, watching television, listening to the radio (if the prisoner can afford to purchase a TV and radio), writing letters to family, friends, and overworked lawyers, and studying law."

Death Row, not unlike any other part of the prison system is tattered with a diverse group of individuals and there is no single all-inclusive description that can be fairly applied to every man condemned to die. While it is true that there are some egregiously dangerous prisoners that have been condemned to death, this is the exception rather than the rule. As there are exceedingly more serial killers and prisoners convicted of multiple homicides serving life sentences or less time in the general population of State and Federal prisons throughout the US or A. Some of the prisoner on Death Row proclaim their innocence outright, some are victims of circumstance, other are prisoner guilty of homicide, but not guilty of first-degree murder, still not being fortunate enough to have knowledgeably qualified and experienced trial attorneys—they have been wrongly convicted of first-degree murder, and subsequently wrongly sentenced to death. From day to day one can lie back on his bunk and listen to one legal horror-story after another of all the injustice that goes on and one must suffer.

Being human, Death Row prisoners also can have a sense of humor and may spend an afternoon "kickin' the bobo", that is, jocularly teasing and jesting with one another. Over time one can come to know, like, and enjoy a genuine friendship with a fellow inmate, albeit in the back of one's mind he may never know whether this friend was once capable of murder, or if he did not do it to start with. So one always has to keep a guard up.

It is commonly argued that Death Row inmates are the worst of all criminal elements of our society. Such a suggestion is mere propaganda. Ideally, the death penalty was to be carefully and deliberately used, appallingly, today's death row prisoner might get someone who accidentally shot someone with a gun believed to have been unloaded, or a school kid who has foolishly and ignorantly thrown his life away by taking someone else's life in a fit of anger or in a dare, or just out right innocent.

What has out country's men and women gone to to let so much injustice to go on in our courts today? What are we say to our children that will one day run this country? It's okay to be unjust and the more money they have the more unjust they can be.

John himself wrote concerning the hardships of those confined to a life waiting for death, a life where the water does not slake the thirst, food does not satisfy the hunger and fear prevails. The guards who are supposed to maintain order and combat chaos, he believes, are responsible for violent beatings and even the same crime for which he was convicted: murder. John even goes so far as to suppose that the guards and staff are trying to create a maelstrom of discontent in order to create chaos so that they have justification for more violence aimed at the inmates. John then asks what this sort of situation says about this type of society.

*"I've been pretty much without cold water now for two weeks. Yeah, and it's the middle of summer. To my knowledge 3 work orders have been put in on it by three different sergeants. Luckily I have good neighbors who will fill up a few caps for me when I need it. Hopefully maint. [maintenance] will be here this week to fix it... I just had a thought... maybe all of these changes to the rules around here are designed to get "us" to react negatively, that way the Lt. can "quale" an emergency on death row and get another promotion. It sounds like some of the slimy stuff that goes on in the D.O.C. You wouldn't believe some of the stuff that goes on behind these walls topped with razor wire you see as you drive past them. Heard about the juvenile that was basically beaten to death (or beaten and left to die) at the "bootcamp" prison here in the state. The kid needed medical attention and even though the nurse was there he still died. The video actually shows the kid on the ground, guards standing around him along with the nurse. What happened? Nothing really. Just another day in prison. I'm telling you if they treated animals like this they would be sent to prison for abuse/cruelty. Public opinion would shout for justice, but for a prisoner... nothing. Barely a ripple or a whisper. What does this say about society?"*

John's question is a valid one. What kind of a society would preach kindness and benevolence and then create a penal system that is so arbitrary, so willing to kill without any sense of the things that John believed in, like honor, glory or fame. No, this is a cold and harsh environment that is a factory for death and the inmates are little more than slaughterhouse cattle mewing and bleating their final pleas for mercy to the Gods. In the old days, when a supposed injustice was done, the person was put on trial, as in the person had to complete a task that was, granted, virtually impossible, like the Labors of Hercules: Juno was mad at Hercules and put him in a blind, furious rage (not unlike that of John who claimed he only remembered walking into the woods that night and nothing afterwards). Hercules killed his wife and children. When he regained his senses, he realized what he had done and he was given his labors to complete, stealing valuable objects and killing dangerous monsters. And he did so, by any means available to him. But, there is no such poetry in this Modern World, only tedium and the stench of rotting fear and impending doom. There is no hope.

71

*"Oh, we hear about it when an inmate is coming up for execution. The day that the governor signs a death warrant we hear about it. Or within a couple of days. Since they went through with Grossman's execution we are figuring that the governor will be signing another warrant soon. I did not know Grossman. I saw him around but never talk to him. When someone does get executed it does weigh heavy on everyone's mind. Because it means a friend in some case is gone and it means that someone else will be next. And no one will know who it will be until a warrant is sign. It's like someone that has cancer. They know they will die any day but don't know when. Since I've been on death row there has been five inmates executed that I had got to know. It's like losing a family member because guys in here become family. It is hard. What scares the hell out of me, [the state] has executed at least four innocent men that I knew so far since 1986. I may be innocent but still set here with the thought that I could be executed.*

*It is also a world without irony or depth. Punishment is sheer and brutal. In the Old Days, for instance, Tantalus was judged by the gods for stealing ambrosia and nectar from their banquet table and revealing the secrets of the Gods; later he cut up a youth named Pelops and served him to the Gods as a sacrifice, but the Gods were horrified at having been served human remains. They cast Tantalus to the underworld, where he was always hungry and always thirsty, yet each time he reached for the fruit hanging above him, it receded and each time he bent to drink the water beneath him, it ran away. Thus, he was Tantalized for his sins. In this Modern World, there is no poetry. The underworld is even darker, harsher and crueler than the world above. This Hades is called "confinement".*

*I will be glad to see Tuesday morning get here. These 30 days on confinement has done me. When they move me off confinement Tuesday morning I will be going to five wing, bottom floor... When I came to confinement I weighed 202 to 205 lbs. Last Sunday they checked everyone's weights. I weight 170 lbs. So I've lost 30 to 35 lbs. In the first three weeks. For the past two weeks I have just had no energy to do anything. So I am sure I've lost more the past week. I have eaten everything on every tray I got too. I am praying that 5 wing will be like 2 wing was. When I as on 2 wing I was always able to get at least 2 or 3 extra trays a day because guys who get canteen every week don't eat some of the State food and would always give it to me. I'm praying that it will be like that on 5 wing. Because if I can't pick up a couple of trays from others my butt is in trouble as far as food goes. I may have to get written up so I can come back to confinement. The problem with that is. There are only a few cells that are open.*

*Some insist that the food is filled with deadly carcinogens that eat away at the organs and kill prisoners from the inside out; most just complain that there is not enough food and that the food that is slid into their cells three times a day is horrible. Inmates often trade their food trays for cigarettes, gambling that the smoke of tobacco is healthier than whatever is on that tray. Worst of all, prisoners do not know what it is they are supposed to consume when it comes to them.*

*The struggle to keep one's sanity through all of this year in and year out is quite a battle in itself, as we watch friends and loved ones die around us each year. Many times we have to deal with money hungry lawyers and investigators that only break their promises of freedom and steal what little money they can squeeze out of you and your family members. When you're already limited resources are depleted you are no longer able to help yourself or fight for your freedom, there is no time for normal life or relationships in this place of hell. There is no time to even dream of a life after prison if we are released. The only goal we allow ourselves to consider is the hope of a new trial or reduced sentence so that we can one day have freedom once again. Even then we will always be faced with being accused of a serious crime. This mountain of injustice must be removed. If it can only be removed one stone at a time then we will die with a stone in our hands.*

*I managed to find a small light in the corner of my cell. I pulled it on and saw to my horror that what I had been eating was covered in blood. I was not sure if it was my own or someone else's. My hunger and my will to survive grew stronger... I had to eat and I finished eating with tears running down my face, while screaming inside, "What kind of place is this!" Only later did I find out that a young man had been killed in the kitchen that morning by another prisoner and it was his blood that I had eaten. Upon hearing that news I began to vomit and could not eat for several more days. After my first meal on death row I managed to get back to sleep while silently listening to the sounds of 100 men on death row begin their day. They were sounds I had never heard before from so many people, coughing, sickness, screaming, even laughter. Smoke and death filled the air and it felt as if every man was slowly dying a horrible death.*

*The jailer's and the court of law's edicts are based on the Bible and the laws that say one must die if one is found to be a killer. But even here, the jailer contradicts his precious Bible where it says: "But flesh with the life thereof, the blood thereof, shall ye not eat." (Genesis 9:4) "For it is the life of all flesh; the blood of it is for the life thereof: therefore I said unto the children of Israel, Ye shall eat the blood of no manner of flesh: for the life of all flesh is the blood thereof: whosoever eateth it shall be cut off." (Leviticus 17:14) It's a cruel, base irony that this Biblical Law should be perverted as such and literally crammed down the throats of the inmates."*

John continued his Path in prison under these horrible circumstances. His Path became a more cerebral one; the wandering was no longer physical – no more visions of wolves in the wilderness of Wyoming. Instead, it was more like the solitary hermit locked in the cave of some great mountain, studying the ancient text filled with wisdom. When those were devoured, John consumed the works of newer masters who tried to figure out the human psychology and the experts on Eastern religions like Buddhism. He still extolled the virtues of the Old Ways to which he was dedicated. Outside of the glaring and dangerous contradictions he saw in Christianity and its doctrines, John, like so many great thinkers, began to see that there were similarities: the Book of Psalms could be seen as an ancient text of prayers and incantations; myths converged; what Christians called 'prayer', Pagans called 'ceremony'; the basis of all religions were to fulfill our unseen, spiritual side. As a true Pagan, John did not judge or persecute the Christians (as he had been) but was still rankled by his people having been harmed. Still, he saw value in many different things, traditions, ways and people – both Modern and Old.

John, of course, saw little more than inaccuracy and contradiction in this Bible that his jailers held so dear. He questioned the inbreeding of Adam, Eve and their offspring and wondered why and how incest could be against God's Law if his original offspring engaged in the act. Then, he believed, in general, there was no Law. He had been judged and thrown into a synthetic underworld based on mankind's interpretation of Divine Law.

*"Why is it that incest is against God's word? Then there is no law... That was probably the beginning of my path to becoming a pagan. When my parents divorced I stayed with my mother and she and I began to associate with other pagans. Now Pagans and Neopagans, as well as Wicca, generally don't brainwash their kids, thinking that everyone should be free of undue influence to choose his own belief system. Oh, I was initiated into the religion in my late teens. However, I did do a self-dedication ritual when I was 14 years old [the dedication to Herne which marked him with great violence], so you might say I've been a pagan or 28 years, 5 months and 28 days. My self-dedication ritual was not like the initiations and rituals we would find in the majority of pagan groups. For one, I swore a blood oath to remain true to my path and I have. There is no real sacrifice such as this, and as such, few hold true to their convictions. I think if it was required to shed blood on the altar, swearing in oath that asks the gods to destroy you if you fell or faltered on the path more people would stick with it. My personal opinion, of course, of what attracted me to it as because it wasn't like the other beliefs I have encountered. No inherited guilt. No shame-based controls. No contradictions that made no sense and no sense of my way or no way; if it ain't like us it is evil. And no God casting people in eternal torment pain and etc.*

*for disagreeing. But he's a loving god. Instead, paganism said we are truly the children of gods and goddesses. And we are gods ourselves, just not mature. We grew up over several hundreds to thousands of lifetimes for reincarnation until we are able to take our place among the Gods. [Pagans] don't say other gods don't exist, but accept they do; they are just not our gods. There isn't 'some do and don't do this' and no black and white philosophy. Life isn't simple, and for a deity to set down roles in stone that cannot address all problems only leads me to think the majority of religion of the mainstream as more of a creation of man and not from a divine being. [Paganism is] one thing above all of this is: the connection with nature, the knowledge of the supernatural that we as children of gods, we can shape local reality to where it is what some might call witchcraft. Other religions tend to call it a prayer. Some of the ideas in my personal philosophy is that there is no absolute, no good or evil. Life and death is pretty much the same thing; nature trumps artificially created laws and all religion that places a man outside of nature. And [nature] does not. Almost all of the species of this planet form one biosphere; as such, we are one extended family and a part of the whole. No single species can be singled out and placed above or below the other. In European terms, [the term "Pagan"] covers perhaps five or six major groups, and each one of those has up to as many 10 subgroups, each having their own little differences. In Wicca, there are many different sects. One is called Diannic Wicca, which is all female-- no men allowed. Though male children of members are [allowed], if they are yet to enter puberty at times, and then not allowed even then. There are even more modern types called Techno-Pagans, who were so sometimes conduct rituals online. Rumor has it that there are a few covens operating in World of Warcraft and Second Life.*

*My own grandmother converted to Christianity, most likely to please my grandfather. Or perhaps it was to hedge her bets near the end of her life. In either case, she would watch Jim Baker's 700 club ministries and send donations in. I once told her that the guy is a fraud and not to waste your money, but she continued to donate. When he was arrested by the feds, I didn't say a word. Anyone on TV asking for money, I looked upon with more than a healthy measure of skepticism. Especially a religious group. At one time, I wrote to a guy in South Carolina who had done a missionary work in China. He relied completely on God to not only fund missionary work, but also his family now in the U.S. I gave him many ideas to make money and each time he came back with the same time God will see us through. Sorry, but I had to stop writing him because he was an idiot. What made him an idiot in my eyes? 'cause he and his wife continued to breed like rabbits though he had no way to provide for the offspring. There is an old Arabic proverb, "Trust in god but tie your camel tight." I think that says it all. A god helps those who help themselves first. Yeah, like you, I couldn't stomach the obvious contradictions that peppered the Bible. One is actually a matter of doctrine and not scripture that brings the idea of grace and the popular interpretation that Christians fall outside the Judaic laws. This is actually attributed to [Jesus'] saying, "I've not come to do away with the laws"; for me, that means the laws still apply. Have you heard these laws? The one that really irks me is the one that states that if someone has sex with your daughter, even by force, and she doesn't call for help and she becomes his wife, he has to pay the father 50 shekels as a bride price for the female. I'm confronted with many people with that one. In my belief, the rapist is in for a bad day, though we don't think of things such as sex in the same way as Christians do. Or for that matter the rest of the monotheistic religions. It's not that the guy had sex with her or about premarital sex. It's about forcing her to do so. But then I tend to have much different morals."*

John knew the value of blood, and how "blood calls to blood." In ceremonies, it is sacrificed as the life force of existence, that which sustains life. Numerous times John would emphasize the need to consecrate a vow in blood in order to harden words that are all too often thrown about carelessly and without meaning. For Pagans, blood had sacred significance; for Christians, especially the early Hebrews, blood was anathema, outlawed from the diet. Even today, a kosher diet has to drain the blood from the animals it is to slaughter. This is because Lilith and Cain, as well as their offspring preyed on blood for immortality, and in the Christian view there was only one Immortal, God himself. John, however, having begun his true Path with a blood oath, saw a crucial flaw in not revering blood, most clearly in the symbolic Blood of Christ represented by wine and the figurative Flesh of Christ represented by a wafer. In fact, John says that this symbolic ceremony as opposed to an actual ingestion of blood, drains power from the individual, leaving them, and the masses around them submissive and subservient to a god floating in the sky; a god, moreover, that was taken from earlier Sumerian and Babylonian traditions.

*"I think if people actually had to eat flesh and drink blood, they would go find a different religion. However, there were rituals in ancient times that did exactly that; they chose a person and for a period of time usually a year [they were] were treated like a god. Then at the end of the prescribed time, they were killed. That gave way to the sacrificial animal, which in turn gave way to sacrificing of grains and goods. Now we sacrifice money as the offering plate is passed around. I wonder who had the stronger faith. The concept of Heaven and Hell, I think, were created by priest to use as a way to control the people. The early Catholic Church turned into one [a way to control people] via the idea of excommunication, combined with being the only conduit to god. Add to this the confessional to get the goods on people to make blackmailing people easy and you have complete control.*

*True, there are historical facts in the Bible and it does lend some validity to it. However, many writers weaved actual fact into their works even though, as a whole, it's fiction. My vampire books use actual places and historical fact to give the reader something to connect with. The entire story is fiction. I can't believe that this trick is new. As for the stories in the Bible being true, recall the game called Gossip; some call it Telephone. The line of 10 or 20 people in a line and you tell a story to one person on the end. That person presents it to the next and so on until the last person is told. They recite the story aloud and check it against the original. The outcome is that certain acts remained intact while the essence of it has now changed. Compound this by hundreds, if not thousands of years, and you get a wild story with a few facts.*

*The art of witchcraft, or what some called The Craft, is not all incantations, though the spoken word is important. Many pray for what they want. For Pagans, we try to create change not only to asking a God for it, but also trying to impose our will on reality to bring about the desired outcome. Many pagans and others call the Book of Psalms represents a Judaic collection of spells, as most ancient incantations are chanted... By using herbs and other minerals, we mix cook, distill etc., various things for a virtual cornucopia of uses. Before being arrested, I had a 4-inch binder literally filled with uses for various herbs and minerals, as well as many recipes for everything from antiseptic to wood sealers. I lost all of that as my landlady was a Christian and either destroyed or sold off everything left there. Isn't the first time information of mine was destroyed. As you can imagine, I have a very special place in my thoughts for small-minded people.*

*True that I prefer a more classical approach to many things. I'm also a modernist in other areas. Let's say I enjoy taking the best of both worlds of the classical ancient and the modern to combine them. Or to reuse a well worn adage, 'Those who forget the past are doomed to repeat it.' One of the reasons why I think we should hold onto the past is that so many in modern society have become weak and soft and without meaningful direction. True, there are many aspects of the ancient world that has no place in today's world, but much of today's way of doing business, dealing with life's complex issues, seem to make little or no sense. Thus, the ideology that brought about the usage of "political correctness." Let's be honest here, the practice of "political correctness" is merely a way to obfuscate real issues and the truth of the reality of a situation. It's not really about being nice because we still think what we think about certain situations; it's not about expressing diversity within a particular group, no; it's just a way to reach other in the most planned way we can imagine.*

*The new religion of Christianity certainly co-opted the old Pagan holidays. Even more, they have stolen much of the imagery from the old religion. The upcoming holiday of Easter that celebrates the rising from the dead of their Christ. The name is derived from a Germanic goddess Oestara or Oster, and her festival, which falls on the spring equinox around March 21. The symbol of this goddess is the egg and rabbit and [there] was a festival celebrating birth, rebirth, regeneration etc. Certainly, a fertility goddess, which of course flew into the face of [Christianity] and God and the uptight male-dominated and usually sexually repressed religion he represented.*

*I'm familiar with the works of Carl Jung and this concept of universal iconography which he called archetypical. Fact is, as most pagans are brought up with the thirst for knowledge, and the lack of an all inclusive books such as the Torah, New Testament and Koran, we tend to have to read a great deal to gain understanding of not just our beliefs but the world around us that match our interest in general science properties of plants and mineral, and, probably most import of all, ourselves in mind, body and spirit. Not only do I read on such topics as Jung, but also J.B. Ryan, Atkinson, Evans etc. Freud, I tried to avoid as he is has a great deal of issues even though he did try to remain detached from them. Though his work on trance studies does bear reading. I think my favorite theory of Jung's is the "collective consciousness" or what my mother termed the "group mind." Yes, all things are interconnected, or more to the point, interdependent. I've often daydreamed of the "what if's" had paganism and its ideology become the*

*dominant religion. Would we be suffering the same woes the world? Or would we just have different problems to contend with? I know the symbol of the snake slash serpent eating its tail. I can't remember the name which is going to drive me nuts until I can. I just spent like 2 hours looking for it. True the act of surrendering one's worldly power is not so much about redemption; it's about surrendering your power and individuality to the Church. To give them power over you. Some say Jesus was a poor carpenter. Now he wasn't. His uncle was wealthy and took the teenaged Jesus in to learn the business. At least according to one alternate story. Ever wonder why none of his teen and twenty-something years are never told in the approved version of the bible?*

*The philosophy of Buddhism is a valid one and perhaps one without the contradictions. Three monotheistic religions have given us nothing much of real value throughout the ages that has lasted. Buddhism has never been used as an excuse to kill and breed hatred or held us back. The point about Catholicism is that the Dark Ages would have not happened or would have only lasted a couple of hundred years. Then it was the bigotry against [Pagans], the wars against Islam -- not to mention The Inquisition. I have often wondered what the world would be like had we never heard of any of the Big Three. Most likely the Age of Enlightenment and the Age of Reason would have come much sooner. Maybe our technological level would be some 800 years more advanced. Can't say for sure. But we must make do with what we have and build upon that. Hopefully, this will be done with much wisdom, more so than is usually shown today."*

Possibly the greatest torment for John was one that was not planned by anyone of his captors: He was disconnected from Nature. His sister, Kathleen, had taught him early on that ceremonies in their Way needed contact with Nature and a degree of nudity. At least the feet should be bare and in contact with the earth beneath them. Many Pagan ceremonies in the past had been conducted fully nude which was branded by the Church as sexual and lewd in nature; thus, the Church came up with its many bans and puritanical views on the flesh. The flesh, however, was natural and not to be despised. It was part of the grand matrix of the world, as

79

John represented in his the art he scrawled, transformed into cards and sent from his prison-cave.

*"The images of the oak are in all four season. Notice to the left top and the bottom is Spring and Winter the time of the Holly King and Winter, and the right side is Summer and Fall, the time of the Oak King. The Four Seasons are representative of the year and a clock or sun-wise rotation. It incorporates the four lesser Sabbaths of the solar festivals, solstices and equinoxes. And knot-work arms branching from the center circle denotes the greater Sabbaths and Beltane, Lughnassadh and Samhain. Or it can be read the other way, as some pagans do. In either case, it comes out to be for greater and for lesser Sabbaths. The pentagram or pentacle represents several things that you have listed here in your letter, plus the five elements. A cycle of nature Birth and death and rebirth is a core belief of pagans. An unending cycle, an unbroken circle that has no beginning and no end. But the knot-work that makes up the border can be seen as the path of life moving, intertwining, linking and connecting. No one is ever an island unto themselves. The pentacle also represents the five catch phrases of the occult. To know, to dare, to will, to keep silent (or to use the five words: noscere, velle, tocere, audere, ire). Yes I wrote only four catch phrases; if you wish to know all five I've given you the five words to guide you.*

*What anger against a supposedly wrong doing could it be? Could it be the Inquisition may be? Some 300 years of persecution and murders by those of the Christian and later Islamic religions and well over 100,000,000 dead globally.*

*Ire in paganism means anger. Yeah I would it say that could indeed raise someone's ire. Then there's that piss-poor apology by the Pope several years ago. Well that does get me a bit pissed off. Though the Catholic Church weren't the only ones involved in this butchery. I have to say if they ever invent time travel, I'm going to go back to take out Abraham and Moses and the rest at birth in order to save several hundreds of millions of people from being senselessly killed in the name of monotheism.*

*Look first Christians come along into Pagan Europe and 90% of the people there think they're nice enough, if strange having only one god. So to win more converts, they start adopting the nicer gods and goddesses by making them saints, and over time they become part and parcel of the religious methods of the Church. For 1400 years or so, all is well, and then the Martin Luther and all of them break away from Rome. Over the next hundred years or so, people divide into sects, and the Reformation Era is in full swing. Now it is the 21st century and the Fundamentalists needing to be eternal party poopers, much like the Puritans, who were not so pure of heart or steadfast to the Word, wish to have an enemy. Up pops Neo-Paganism, the fastest growing belief system in America, and now anything that was originally Pagan to begin with is now evil incarnate. If we really wish to delve into this line of thought:*

*1. Christians believe Lucifer is the Devil and thus also Satan with the title of prince of lies. He is foretold to take up the guise of religion to fool the people. Right?*

*2. Christian mythos of Jesus is simply the retelling of a much older mythology of very Pagan origins. The God Mithras -- and about four or five other spellings of it -- precedes Christianity by an easy 500 to 1000 years by historical accounts, probably predates the writing of the Torah.*

*3. Satan, a bastardized version of God in Egypt that was seen as a not so-nice god of the Egyptian GOT SET HEN generally known by the vulgar SET.*

*4. The term "sin" -- the Jews were held captive in Babylonian Empires, at the temple of the god SIN-AUP-TU (think that's still the correct way to spell it) Lord of the Moon and Night, when evil prowled the world and lust and violence and murder were the rule. This is also when on Sin's holidays the temple prostitutes of Ishtar would visit the temple of Set for carnal pleasures. Hence the corruption of "sin". The wages of sin is death. Or anyone to be found in the Temple of Sin was to be banished from the Jewish community as if they were dead.*

*5. Scholars believe the Torah was first written in Babylon.*

*6. A god, Yahweh, is actually a local/tribal deity of Midian, which was adapted by the Hebrews early on. They were once just as polytheistic as anyone else. Have no other god before me. Translation: worship me first above all gods, and then you may worship them.*

*Do you think I judge them too harshly? Perhaps pronounce judgment too swiftly? Recall it was the same types who for 300 years hunted down and murdered my ancestors in that religious self -righteous fervor. If you include the indigenous natives of the Americas, this Inquisition killed over 300,000,000 a day by their partners in homicide, rape pillage and plunder subjugating conquered peoples for slaves. This is the foundation of Christianity and the Church as well as the breakaway sects... Go to any missionary and poor countries where they prey on the poor. Food? Convert. Medical aid? Convert. Orphans? Brainwash. Turns my stomach. If they do good for goodness alone, why try to convert them? Yes it a touchy subject, and I allow my hackles to rise for it too easily when confronted with such blatant stupidity. But worse yet, it is the people who gobble up the shit they are shelling out with a simple thought and go back for more. These are the mindless minions of monotheism."*

In the Christian Bible, more specifically in Deuteronomy 22:13-21, the sexual mores of that religion are put on display, namely the fascination with virginity, or physical purity in terms of commercial value. This is another contradiction John thought was confounding; another ancient relic that did not make sense in any decent ideology:

"13If a man takes a wife and, after lying with her, dislikes her 14and slanders her and gives her a bad name, saying, "I married this woman, but when I approached her, I did not find proof of her virginity," 15then the girl's father and mother shall bring proof that she was a virgin to the town elders at the gate. 16The girl's father will say to the elders, "I gave my daughter in marriage to this man, but he dislikes her. 17Now he has slandered her and said, 'I did not find your daughter to be a virgin.' But here is the proof of my daughter's virginity." Then her parents shall display the cloth before the elders of the town, 18and the elders shall take the man and punish him. 19They shall fine him a hundred shekels of silver and give them to the girl's father, because this man has given an Israelite virgin a bad name. She shall continue to be his wife; he must not divorce her as long as he lives. 20If, however, the charge is true and no proof of the girl's virginity can be found, 21she shall be brought to the door of her father's house and there the men of her town shall stone her to death. She has done a disgraceful thing in Israel by being promiscuous while still in her father's house. You must purge the evil from among you."

Leviticus 20:10 and Deuteronomy 22:22 both go on to outlaw free love, restrict carnal relations and virtually outlaw the "green wood" weddings John remembered nostalgically from his days as a practicing Pagan during the days of Beltane:

If a man commits adultery with another man's wife--with the wife of his neighbor--both the adulterer and the adulteress must be put to death.

"If a man is found sleeping with another man's wife, both the man who slept with her and the woman must die. You must purge the evil from Israel."

Sexual relations, especially those outside the sanctimony of a Christian wedding, were deemed evil. When the persecution of the Pagans began in full swing under the Roman Empire and then later the Catholic Church, these sexual ideals were used to outlaw many of the practices of the Pagan faithful. The nudity that was crucial to a connection with the natural world was deemed as demonic, as witchcraft; the sexual congress that was connected to fertility rites, as on the May Day, was deemed immoral "fornication." Sex for pleasure, in fact, was generally looked down upon because it did not produce offspring; sex was always and only to "go forth and multiply." John, had a more indulgent and sensual idea of sex and reproduction, one that was shame-free.

*"Fact is if I get out of here, I'd like to have at least five girlfriends to procreate with. Before I was arrested, I had three fulltime girlfriends, 1 part time girlfriend and a hook-up when she came into town and one that was around for when I got the eye for sex. Now all of them knew about each other; two were actually friends with benefits. Yes, they were bisexual females, which I prefer, and April actually brought Brenda over for sex threesomes. I thought to go for two every day of the week, but realize I needed time off for myself so settled on just five. Figure if I have 3 to 5 children with each, I will be happy, twins and triplets would be a bonus. As for my wanting to make so much money to have so many girlfriends and wives and children, I'd have to make around 200,000 a year now just to support them at a middleclass level. So to afford them at the upper-middle class to mid-range upper class level are only to clear at least 10,000,000 a year... I would decorate my house in object d'art in the study of the nude form from birth to grave -- as it is perfectly natural, from leisure to work, from innocence to play to carnal congress. From sketches, paintings, carvings to castings of bronze inside and out. The Christians would freak if they saw it and would denounce me as the embodiment of Evil, when, in fact, it is they who are so. They claim Original Sin as their own so they are born in sin. I am not. I am without sin for there is no such concept in my belief system. One could argue that because I am not born with Original Sin and I carry none of the shame of their Adam and eve. My life is shame free."*

In Exodus 22:18, the Bible swears death for those who practice magic: "18Do not allow a sorceress to live."

So does Leviticus 20:27:

"A man or woman who is a medium or spiritualist among you must be put to death. You are to stone them; their blood will be on their own heads."

In Acts 8:18–22, there is the story of a man named Simon who wanted to purchase the spiritual power of magic and was threatened with his own death, unless he were to repent and submit to the Lord for forgiveness:

"Now when Simon saw that the Spirit was bestowed through the laying on of the apostles' hands, he offered them money, 19saying, "Give this authority to me as well, so that everyone on whom I lay my hands may receive the Holy Spirit." 20But Peter said to him, "May your silver perish with you, because you thought you could obtain the gift of God with money! 21"You have no part or portion in this matter, for your heart is not right before God. 22"Therefore repent of this wickedness of yours, and pray the Lord that, if possible, the intention of your heart may be forgiven you."

In Deuteronomy 10-14, occult practices, not just magic is forbidden and those who practice such methods will be "driven out' by the Lord:

"There shall not be found among you anyone who makes his son or his daughter pass through the fire, one who uses divination, one who practices witchcraft, or one who interprets omens, or a sorcerer, 11or one who casts a spell, or a medium, or a spiritist, or one who calls up the dead. 12"For whoever does these things is detestable to the Lord; and because of these detestable things the Lord your God will drive them out before you. 13"You shall be blameless before the Lord your God. 14"For those nations, which you shall dispossess, listen to those who practice witchcraft and to diviners, but as for you, the Lord your God has not allowed you to do so."

The ban on witchcraft and Occult and Pagan practices was implemented, quite frankly, because it would spread the power of the Lord, his "magical powers" of resurrection, for instance, and would be solely His. John's Pagan belifs led him to believe that each human is a God in a state of evolution, a God-Becoming, constantly revealing new layers of His/Her powers with each new step along His/Her path. Thus, anyone could become as powerful as God or the Christian Lord given enough reincarnations, dedication and devotion to the Craft, as John calls it. In fact, all of the most important practices, from divining the movements of the stars and the moon and the sun to the individual practice of "casting" spells or shaping the Will to create a reality around the individual, were outlawed and associated with Cain, the "prototype" of the evil man and Lilith, the original woman before Eve who would not submit to the male aggression of Adam. Thus, from the Old Times on, John's people were persecuted and driven from their homes for the time-honored knowledge they held secret to themselves, such as the true nature of the celestial movements and the means of casting suggestive magic.

*"The importance of timing in the occult is that every hour of the day is linked to the planets, just as each part of the year is separated into 12 houses of the zodiac. In a dualistic system, you have a positive and negative aspect to everything -- day and night good and bad etc. In some cultures, the sun is seen as a light-giving source, while in others the sun is a dealer in death and destruction ... Same with the Moon, yes, there are specific rites and spells that call for very specific items or objects to be attained. A Voodoo doll or gris is often made from cloth which has been worn and not washed by the person it is to represent. Aside from herbs, it is generally filled with fingernail clippings, hair, spit, blood etc. from that person, even a picture or sample of handwriting. A doll with all these things in it, and in the right hands, can be a powerful object to heal or kill as one desires. To make a charm of the same sort is as follows: The pairing of nails. Collect spittle and so forth of your intended victim to represent every part of his*

84

*person and then make them up into his likeness with wax from a deserted bee's comb. Scorch the figure slowly by holding it over a lamp every night for seven nights. It is the liver heart and spleen of my victim that I scorch. After the seventh time burned, the figure and your victim will die. This charm obviously combines the principles of homeopathic and contagious magic, since the image which is made in the likeness of an enemy contains things which once were in contact with him, namely his nails hair and so forth. If the above ritual was started on a Full Moon, the subject of could claim to have been under the influence of the spell to carry out the death of the victim in some cases... Yes, a novice would be required to carry out the wishes of the leader of the group to not only prove himself, but to create a blood-type to the group. As for doing some dirty work to cut his teeth, this happens in gangs all the time."*

John demonstrated how to cast a protective space, something that would have garnered death for him in Biblical Times, according to the Bible.

*"The casting of a protective space is usually a circle. It is actually simple, though the Wiccans and Neo-Pagans tend to make it a ritual unto itself. Not necessary. Think of a ring of blue-white energy or flame that begins in the north of the circle and with a stake, staff or sword, you trace a circle into the dirt, as you do so, you see and feel this energy leaving your hand, traveling down the tool and becoming part of the ground, its flames rising higher and higher, creating a dome over your head when you complete the circle. It's important to mark the circle as once you have created the barrier, you should not cross it. Outside, you can use tape on carpet, chalk on concrete or even rope. Outside you can use sticks, stones or make a line in the dirt. When I do this in a place I feel is secure, I will often make the cairn of stones three feet high and place a bowl of earth on the north cairn, place hot coals on the east cairn to burn leaves and herbs for incense, build a fire on the south cairn and place a bowl of water on the west cairn. I also mark out my circle in stones, carving a ruin, sigil and other symbols of protection on them. River stones work well and a cold chisel works well in making remarks.*

*The ritual:*
*Starting at the north part of the circle you cast your search. Once done, you approach the cairn at the east point taping your stick, staff or sword three times on the stones and say...*
*'I call on to the powers of Air! Attend! Aid me this night!'*
*Move to the south cairn, tapping three times saying...*
*'I call upon the powers of fire! Attend! Aid me this night!'*
*Move to the west cairn, tapping three times saying...*
*'I call upon the powers of water! Attend! Aid me this night!'*

*Move to the north cairn, tapping three times saying...*
*'I call upon the powers of earth! Attend! Aid me this night!'*
*Move to the center, still facing north, arms raised above the head,*
*saying...*
*'Hear me, I will keep faith until the earth opens and swallows me.'*
*Turn to the east and say*
*''til the sky falls and crushes me'*
*Turn to the south and say*
*'Until the fire rages and can sue as me.'*
*Turn to the west and say*
*'Until the seas are rise and overwhelms me.'*
*Turn back northward, lifting eyes skyward*
*'With truth in my heart, strength in my hands, consistency on my tongue,*
*By blood, bone and sinew I so swear.'*

*This done, you have called upon the elementals and made a sort of pact with them. It should not be taken lightly, for to break faith with them is to invite trouble from all corners. This is what many don't understand. Those who dabble think they can simply walk away. But just like in a ritual, you go through a Baptism into Christianity, the immersion ritual of Zoroastrianism or passing through the Seven Gates of Walking in the ancient Sumerian religion, these are oaths and are binding. Not just through some unseen, outside power, but within the deep recesses of your own psyche.*

*Anyway, you are ready to tap into the power that surrounds you -- around you, above you, and below you. Reach out, ignoring the five senses of the physical and concentrating on your perceptions beyond the Prima Firma. Fell the Life Energy in everything – tree, insect, animal, earth, stone fire, atom, electron ... all the way down into the quantum level. It flows through everything, through you as well. It moves on all levels of reality, equally crossing the brains between dimensions. Let your nonphysical self touch it, slowly drawn together like so many wisp of smoke, a tangible smoke that comes with energy. Pull at it. Let it flow into you, build inside, wrap around you, infuse you. Form your thoughts into an image, a desire, let that become words, fill those words with your will, your intent, your emotions, your desires, and your full will. Allow the energy to flow through you, shaping it directly with your will. And when it feels as if you must release and send forth the power or faint, you speak the words while keeping your intentions firmly in place.*

*'My will be done!'*

*Then on that last word, you release it, sending it forth to shape reality to your will. Thus the spell is done. Smother the coals on the east cairn and with the earth from the north cairn, and douse the fire in the south with the water from the west cairn. Break the barrier and walk away."*

The individual will that John released in his personal rituals and ceremonies was a grain of sand in a much larger, even cosmic, sort of struggle between forces of Light versus Darkness, supposed "good" versus supposed "evil". John, having studied and immersed himself studies of the old texts and myths saw an age-old battle between forces that manifest in this world but resonate to other planes and dimensions. The traces of this battle and these combatants can be seen in everything from the layout of our greatest American cities, the structure of our political systems and, of course, the precepts of codified religion. Still, John insists, it is the individual that invests meaning into this phenomenon of existence form the inside out, not a God who fills us with meaning from the with a touch of the hand from the Heavens above.

*"Terms Satanic or Satanist is really only one small group of people and they tend to be the shock troops and media cannon fodder. These are the groups you find in Jerry Springer or are trooped out on Halloween specials for the masses. Call them the front men and women of the ideology, to make it all seem silly, disorganized and generally harmless. I direct you now to the net and your search engine to look up the Temple of Set, which is an offshoot of the Church of Satan founded by Anton Lavey, a more serious group and a group that is connected with and the halls of power. But there is still nothing compared to Luciferians. Luciferians are exactly what they claim to be but are intentionally made up of the power brokers in both politics and by national arenas. They recruit members much like the Order of the Skull and Bones, initiating the younger members from the elite, the intelligent, the up and coming. Their philosophy is Christian-based and they use the Bible as a semi-accurate record of propaganda from the great enslaver, i.e. god. They claimed a Yahweh made Adam and the woman Eve as the perfect slaves to blindly worship Yahweh, and so sustain him and his power. Lucifer got Eve to eat of the Tree of Knowledge and was about to get them, Adam and Eve, to eat of the fruit of the Tree of Life so mankind would become Gods -- and his supporters prevented this. The curse laid on mankind, note He (God) refers to Adam and Eve as "livestock", so they were considered nothing better than cattle by Yahweh. He was to keep mankind from being able to rise up against him, forcing them to toil in the earth and suffer through life. Luciferians teach their members that we are gods not just immortal. Then we humans are powerful in and of ourselves, but the Christians and Jews give their power to Yahweh through this worship. If they were to stop then, Yahweh would be reduced in power and Lucifer would win, allowing humanity to*

*finally be free of the yoke of Yahweh. Interestingly enough, there is a group of fanatical Christians who strive for the Apocalypse. This group forced the re-creation of Israel, the continuing support of that nation, and is still trying to bring about the conditions that will sparkle off the last Great War there to bring the Second Coming.*

*The connection of politics and occult is well founded. The Masons conduct ritualized ceremonies. The higher up in the ranks, it becomes even more so. If you look at the layout of Washington, DC, the big monuments and older government buildings, you will see the entire town and city is based on a pattern of geomancy that is occult in its origins. Look at some of the older communities that were designed after the Civil War. The buildings built by some of the more wealthy industrialists. You'll notice some very interesting patterns. Look at the original design of Druid Hills of Atlanta, not what was finally done, but the very beginning designs. These types of places are dotted around the U.S.; they seem to show no real pattern in their overall locations, but they could be situated on mystical ley lines or nodes where two or more ley lines cross, concentrating the power of those particular places.*

*If the group was Satanic or Luciferian, etc., targeting a member of the Catholic Church is a big score. I should point out here that many prominent business persons are not just Christian, Jewish, Muslim etc. There are some Luciferians into big business, as well. Would a leader of a coven who was also a businessman use his power to remove an obstacle from his path? Yes. Especially if he was to gain big time. People are killed by murder or witchcraft for much less all the time. Most covens are not financially secure nor are they led by a businessperson, so as a general rule, that corporate world and occult world or Wicca rarely dance together, but when they do, I should point out that there are many business leaders that consult psychics, card readers etc. They tend to be Non-Pagan themselves. In other countries, however, like in Romania, people often go to the Roma to curse someone they are having difficulty with in their business or personal life.*

*The idea of this confrontation having taken place on the ethereal plane astral plane etc yes does philosophy in the occult is grounded in many cultures doctrines etc. There is actually a form of magic that deals with this. Here you enter the realm and shape your desired affect there. Once put in motion it, translates to this plane of existence. As above so below. Change there and by doing so it creates change from here. However, the more complex you make changes, there is a greater the chance of it failing and collapsing. Another form of this is the idea of each person being represented by a spiritual line or cord this cord intertwines as people come together, interact and then separate and part company. Some say they can manipulate the weaving tapestry of life by moving the spiritual cords to intersect with other eternal struggles. There are archetypical images and situations that continuously play out in the world. Some call it the Great Cosmic Play. Some people think we are subject to the whims and wishes of the gods. An occultist would say something to the effect of not all things can be seen or known. We are influenced day to day by our fellow humans, so why not be influenced by the unseen and subtle stimuli of the smallest things. A fraction of a second either way changes the outcome of our experience. But it is we who give things meaning. We do so to gain some kind of understanding to it all, because we crave to place meaning on things beyond what we see. If there is no greater meaning, then we are merely smart, careless apes on a ball circling a common-type star in a common-type galaxy, floating in the universe, slowly rotting until we die, which only speeds up the process. That is something we as a species cannot accept and will not accept. If this is all there is, no great reward or a hereafter, then why should we hold true to social and religious morals?"*

And John will not hold true to those morals imposed upon him, even if he is locked away in a steel-and-concrete tomb. He will spread his knowledge through the world through letters scrawled in his neat, tight script, inveighing against the powers that doomed him without any sort of irony or poetry; he will continue to cast his protective space from his mind to everywhere around him; he will live as a mind encased in steel, his thoughts bursting out through the metal slats and toward the same sun that washes over all of us. He will persist. And, according to John himself, he will rise and live again…

# Summerland

*"Death solves all problems - no man, no problem."*
Joseph Stalin

*"The disembodied spirit is immortal; there is nothing of it that can grow old or die. But the embodied spirit sees death on the horizon as soon as its day dawns."*
Thomas Hobbes

Christians cast their sinners first to death and then to Hell for eternal torment and damnation. This idea is almost uniquely Christian. The word Hell stems from the Old English word hel or helle which did not imply the torment but simply a world of the dead. In the Anglo-Saxon period the word halja meant "one who covers up or hides something." Even in the belief system of the Norse Pagans, there is a word for Hell, Hel, but it implies no sort of punishment or even flames and brimstones; it is a misty place that houses the dead.

The idea of Hell is for those who believe in a linear history, that time goes in one straight line from beginning to middle to death in the individual sense and the Apocalypse in the biggest sense. John did not believe in Hell, in part because he could see the value in a cyclical history. He believed all the crackpots who were predicting the end of the world in 2012 were not smart enough to see that the Mayan calendar was circular and cyclical. Therefore, the calendar simply started over the same way the stars and the celestial constellation simply moved back to their original positions in the night sky. This is the Return of the Gods, the stars moving back to their original glory where the naked human eye can see them. Just as the stars and planets went in cycles, so did humanity.

*"Now the notion that the gods were highly advanced humans and master scientists is common, and I for one, don't discount it. In fact, by the actions of humans in the last 100 years, I can fully believe that there was an advanced civilization of humans here long ago and they self-destructed. We are what is left, and now we are waltzing down the same primrose path. So, I can also grasp the idea of a cyclical history."*

Thus, there could not be an eternal torment or a permanent place of pain. Time, according to John, was infinite/cyclical and matter/what we are made of is finite, so eventually we had to be reproduced, even after millions of years – every moment would be reproduced eventually. So, how can there be any "good" or any "evil"?

Nonetheless, the Ancient Greeks had a literal underworld where people experienced ironic and almost poetic tormenting for their misdeeds; this could be the beginning of the Christian concept of a subterranean place where sinners are tortured. The Christians, however, created the greatest fear-control methodology ever created: the Hell ruled by The Devil who poked you with his pitch-fork and roasted your Soul over hot flames for all Eternity. As Daniel says in the Bible:

"And many of those who sleep in the dust of the earth shall awake, Some to everlasting life, Some to shame and everlasting contempt."

This figurative idea of Hell was made literal in America; it was shaped out of steel, stone and concrete; it was the American prison system, the place where the will of Christian God can be done "on earth as it is in heaven." So, John was sent to Death Row for his "sin."

Facing death in his steel and concrete cell, locked down 23 hours a day, John, the Pagan on his Path, knew that each tick of the clock was a step toward his own Apocalypse at the hands of the Bible-Belt power-brokers who sought to expel "evil" from their Christian midst. John maintained his path. Though physically restrained, his mind was still allowed to roam free and pursue the knowledge that all Pagans strive for, the ancient truths at the heart of his faith.

Since childhood, John, like so many classical heroes and villains had been banished from society for his beliefs. John had been ripped from one childhood home and dropped in another, torn from his sister's side, tossed to one foster home after another, one state hospital after another; when the young John rode through the night on a purloined bicycle, even his father turned him away. When John questioned the Bible itself, and how incest could possibly be justified, he was kicked out of the church's Sunday school.

Little did John know, however, that he was touching on answers and gathering information in those early, iconoclastic years, which would lead him to the culmination of his Path which was a beginning and an end in itself, like the serpent eating its own tail, constantly dying and being re-born. Facing death at the end of his mortal path, John toyed with ideas of immortality.

The Wiccans believe in a place called Summerland, named after the part of the year when things are grown but still new, just before the presence of death rears its head. This is not a place, however, of Biblical judgment, where the "sinners" burn and the righteous rejoice. Summerland is a place where the newly deceased look at a reflection of themselves, look at what they have done during the previous incarnation and "reflect" on it – changing and improving.

Instead of a deathbed conversion to Christianity to "hedge his bets" as his grandmother had done, or professing a new-found faith in Wicca and its Summerland, John became fascinated with the immortality found in vampires, those blood-drinking creatures of the night who spawn from the first woman, the one who came before Eve, mated with Cain and created a race so powerful, so eerie and immortal that they were shunned from society and bear no mention in the Bible. These are the descendants of Lilith and Cain, the first vampires.

In Genesis 1:27, well before Eve is mentioned in Genesis 2:21, there is mention of Lilith, who was made to be Adam's equal and opposite. Lilith refused to submit to her partner. She insisted on lying on top when they had intercourse; they argued and she, like John, was banished to wander through the barren lands outside of the towns and villages of the ancient world. She was forced to hide her countenance from the light of day, when the righteous could see her and make her doom. She became the she-demon of the night, mentioned in Isaiah 34:14 (her only other mention in the codified version of the Bible) as Lilit, which all at once translates as "night owl," screech owl," "night hag," and of course, "vampire." This story is probably, as John intimated about the Bible as a whole, taken from the Sumerian myth of a woman married to the first man who was banned from him and eventually preyed on mortals. At the same time as this Sumerian myth was told in the ancient world, there was a Roman myth of a female vampire-like creature (associated with owls) that preyed on the blood of the living for immortality. So, Lilith roamed the outlands on her own, a solitary witch, the mother of all demons, killing the newborn until the day of their naming, the seventh day for girls and the eight day for boys, unless the names of the three angels hung over their cribs; or, as the ancient Hebrews wrote over their children on talismans to ward off Lilith: Lilith-abi, which became the English word, lullaby. And so she maintained her vitality.

Then she met Cain, the firstborn of Adam, the first man, and Eve, the second female, made from Adam's rib so that she could never claim equality with him. Eve, even before Cain slew his brother with the jaw-bone of an ass, had a dream of Cain drinking blood, so much blood in fact that it overflowed and ran down his chin, neck and arms. After Cain's murder of his brother, he was expelled to wander in the Land of Nod, where he saw Lilith on the shores of the Red Sea. Lilith brought him into her fold and showed him the power of blood; Eve's premonition had come true.

The unnamed woman in the Bible that Cain has a brood of illegitimate children is Lilith. His children, though outcasts as their father and mother, were known for their inventions and innovations in music and metal working. Cain, expelled to Nod, was also expelled from the Bible and is not mentioned after

Genesis until the New testament, when he is called the "prototype of a wicked man." He appears in the apocryphal books of the Bible but in no such Hebrew books as the Torah. A thousand years later, Christian monks on the Land of Angles (angels?)(John's lineage home) were writing down a long-told bardic tale of dragons, demons, good, evil, gold, fire and ancient lairs; a tale called Beowulf. This is where Cain and his "evil" brood resurface; the "evil" serpents of the Beowulf tale are literally, not figuratively linked to descendants of Cain, and therefore Lilith. In fact, this tale implicates Cain and Lilith for creating every form of inequity, a whole catalog of monsters:

"...Till the monster stirred, that demon, that fiend,
Grendel, who haunted the moors, the wild
Marshes, and made his home in a hell
Not hell but earth. He was spawned in that slime,
Conceived by a pair of those monsters born
Of Cain, murderous creatures banished
By God, punished forever for the crime
Of Abel's death. The Almighty drove
Those demons out, and their exile was bitter,
Shut away from men; they split
Into a thousand forms of evil-- spirits
And fiends, goblins, monsters, giants,
A brood forever opposing the Lord's
Will, and again and again defeated.
(Ll. 101-114)
...Cain had killed his only
Brother, slain his father's son
With an angry sword, God drove him off,
Outlawed him to the dry and barren desert,
And branded him with a murder's mark. And he bore
A race of fiends accursed like their father...
(Ll. 1261-1266)"

This "thousand forms of evil" roamed the earth from the day Lilith and Cain started their brood, but they, unlike the "righteous" Christians who feared them and railed against them, were immortal so long as they satisfied their thirst for blood and found relatively "innocent" vessels to transfer their souls into when their flesh perished. This was the brood of vampires, creatures of the night, screech owls, and shadow stalkers – yet impervious to death – and also John's last hope for eternal life. John described the ceremony by which the vampire maintains life: "The crossing over ceremony… it's a fancy term for funeral. Though it's not like any mainstream funeral ceremony you might attend today. Some traditions do it soon after death. Others: before death and still others wait until Samhain, October 31, or soon after, or on the New or Full Moon, or closer to that date when the veil between the worlds are thin, to perform the ceremony. When it is done before death, it is more about the passage of one generation and passing on the power of that person the next. As much a blessing of the next generation as it is the choosing of the successor of the mantle of power and leadership. In the coven, it is a gathering to honor the person reaching the end of his life and to say goodbye as well as to speed them on to what awaits them. That almost all Pagans are reincarnated, they often times reinforce the spiritual bonds that connect the family/coven so that the spirit-soul of the dying and dead return to the group. In less common events, as it is not widely known, the coven will choose the person within their own ranks to be the vehicle of rebirth; it will always be a woman for she is the grail of creation and so she has the spirit and soul attached to her and goes out to take a mate from within the coven, or from without it in some cases. Some Pagans believe this to be a violation of some Cosmic Law and may be why it is generally not practiced. As for the solitary practitioner, the person can if they are prepared and have attained the knowledge and power and self discipline to do so, complete the right themselves -- choosing a vehicle of rebirth. However there are drawbacks to this by going for the entire birth process in growing up through infancy to toddler. Your Past-Life memories tend to get lost in the less developed brain, being pushed down into the unconscious area of the psyche. For the magi or witch who is not restrained by the moralistic issues, there is a way to avoid the problem and retain the knowledge from this previous life.

The magi having taken the time to go through the needed rituals and conversion of energy, and once separated from the body, seeks out the child between two and five years old that will be the vessel of their spirit soul. It's more akin to possession as the magi -- or witch -- now enters the body and seeks to overwhelm the spirit born into it. The outcome usually is either the young spirit's soul is addicted and the magi or witch takes up residence unimpeded -- or stalemated -- in which the dominant spirit takes control or influence in the original occupant.

*There are instances, of course, when the reincarnated spirit is able to defend against the magi or which, in which case, they have to find an easier host. Find a child who has stopped breathing – then their job is easier. The possession of older people is more difficult as the spirit or soul is well developed and strongly attached to the physical form. However, if the magi or witch can find a freshly dead body still being worked on by medical staff, they can often times take this body or a vehicle or vessel; but here also is a danger, as they would experience that pain and trauma of that host body. And the memories of the host body are oftentimes confusing. Again the past memories can be pushed deep into the subconscious. Ever heard of people who have near-death experiences and wake up and seem to not know their family members, or they speak differently? Sometimes they wake up and are speaking a foreign language all together? I often wonder if these events are not a case of some adept taking up residence in the body.*

John came to know the ways of vampires and could see the differences between the real ones who thirsted for blood and the extension of life it lent them and the phonies, the clowns who masqueraded and made his attempts at resurrection seem like blasts of media hype.

*"The article on John Brennan Crutchley, also known as the vampire rapist, was one I had never heard before. Very interesting case to be sure. Though if he had been as organized as the authorities would have you believe, he would have been caught in the first place. Consider for a moment that he had an excellent job and a fair amount in his paycheck. A closed building, perhaps underground, if it had been anywhere else but coastal areas or a concrete block workshop would work and be cheap to build either on his property or on a remote site. Solid windows, like those glass masonry blocks and a steel door -- call it a hurricane shelter if you will. No chance of escape; a drain in the center for easy cleanup and he would have never been caught. While he may have successful for a time, the truly high functioning and organized serial killers are never caught because they leave nothing to chance, from the choosing of their target to the disposal of the body. An example taken from* Fargo, *the movie: a wood chipper directed over a body of water, a butcher knife and a box of bags (trash), plus a hammer for the skull to make it fit into the chipper. Then use a bit of acid to clean the organics off and out of the chipper. No evidence. This is what a high-functioning serial killer would do. As for victims, the serial killer would choose them from the large homeless and poor, watching and studying the potential target to which or that they had no family or friends who would be able to report them missing. A trip to a soup kitchen is a good place to gather this information. He was an opportunistic predator at best, though successful in that he was able to get away with it for so long. It was only because the victims didn't have any solid connection to him. Face it, police are not all that smart. If the predator is smart enough to never hunt in his own area and avoid the victims who will be noticed missing, they will not be caught unless it is by sheer accident.*

*How do I know this? I have contemplated writing a fictional portrayal of just such a person. Though he does kill, he would not primarily do so, but take*

95

*contracts to locate individuals for others. Matching a person by their characteristics with what's desired, abduct them after studying the targets, and using drugs and electroshock to wipe the individual memory clean to create a blank slate for his clients. But by the end of the book, the reader would find out that he has created his own family by the same process which will mirror him in personality and skills to carry on after him. Or he is caught by witches by accident when his wife is killed. The last part of the book cuts to a minivan, with mom dead and three kids plus teenager, (one mail and slightly younger female) whom the family picks up hitchhiking."*

The book John actually did "craft" was much different, much more to the point of the life of the modern vampire, the raw lust and the need for this plane of existence. Here's the beginning of his hopeful book:

"Greetings!

Where to begin this fateful tale of my life? I have carried the outline of this tome in my head for what seems like an eternity, but now that I have pen in hand and paper beneath it, I find that the words choke and refuse to flow as easily as I anticipated they would. Telling my story is more difficult and emotional than t expected it to be, so I shall merely write to you of how it all began, and how it came to end. Yes...end. For as with all things mortal and ephemeral, my life ended and concluded on the saddest of terms. I exist still! Though, if this is life, then I am truly dammed. But, please, let me start over...

Myself, I shall exist eternally as a vampire; one of the immortals. How tragic these words seem to me now, though all my mortal life I dreamed the imaginary life of a vampire with a romantic fascination. I played at it then. It was an indulged lifestyle I allowed myself to thrive in. I attended grand costumed events and haunted every contrived theme bar I could find in my youth. I dressed only in elegant black, feeling handsome and dashing and sexily evil. And, I went about the night enjoying the company of others who thought as I did, dressed as I did, and who revered the same beloved books of fiction that fueled our fantasies and allowed us an outlet for our most secret of desires. Little did I know at the time that these works of fiction were more telling and truthful than any obscure tome of magic and legend I ever beheld. Yes, I studied the occult. I worked frequently with magic, cast spells and mixed potions. I called and dominated spirits through my knowledge... truly an apt word to use on this occasion. "Knowledge." The combination of "know" and "ledge," for I built within me such a high ledge, a cliff, over the engulfing abyss that I was soon to fall into.

Yet, for all of my supposed knowledge, I was destined to come into my current state of existence in a totally different manner than the traditionally stated methods told in those beloved works of fiction that I had grown to love and revere. I was to discover that there is far more truth than fiction in the works of that most honored writer of vampire novels, my muse, Our Mistress of New Orleans. Yes, there is truth in her words, but not all secrets of the Vampire are revealed in them, I know not whether her writings are works of true fiction created in her own mind or glimpses of the truth taken from the experiences of those such as I, surreptitiously handed over to her to be published in her name. One day when my story has been written, I shall seek her out one night and ask for myself if she will offer my tale to her readers. But then, perhaps not. We shall see.

But, enough of these ramblings... I now sit in an abandoned cottage located somewhere high in the mountains of North Carolina. I go to sleep... Ha! Sleep? I go to my daily death in a damp, hidden cave not far from here, and I take my nourishment from the animals of the forest, although deer hunting is now long out of season, as if that were to matter to one such as I. Can you see me taking the time to apply for a hunting license? Surely my blind hunger for them would take control of me and I would slaughter and ravage all in any establishment I entered. No, I avoid all humans now, unless I am well sated. Unless I have need of them.

But, how did I come to be in this state? How did 1 fall into the world of the vampire? I have pondered this question for many a night, and I now know. As I said, I was one of those reckless youths who played at the dark arts; played at being a creature such as 1 am now. And, in those days I frequented bars and clubs that encouraged role-playing and a gothic lifestyle of decadent wanton pleasures. 1 favored these places, and as all young people do, thought nothing ill could ever befall me. It was in such a place as this that I met Gloria.

To say that she was beautiful would be to say the sky was blue. With human eyes I adored her the moment I sensed her presence; she of wonderfully pale, milky skin and cascading red hair. Her soft tresses framed her delicate face and fell in ringlets across her bare shoulders. Her lips were painted the deepest of reds, and her eyes sparkled with the color of the brightest of emeralds. I fell immediately in love with her.

Many times we played the blood drinker, the vampire, together. I bear the scars on my wrists even now, having been made and healed naturally while 1 was mortal. She drank from me, and I from her many times, on countless occasions. I know they say the sharing of blood is different for each person who experiences it, but for us, for me at least, it was sensual and highly erotic. No, I didn't see visions as many report, unless Gloria was my vision. I drank of her. Her blood. And this sharing was what brought me to be what I am now: a vampire.

I met her in a new club that had just opened in Atlanta called the Cavern. It was one of those trendy spots that pop up overnight and create so much positive word-of-mouth "buzz" through the more established clubs that it's the immediate "in" place to be. Located on a back street near a section of old, abandoned warehouses, the Cavern quickly attracted others like myself, and drew in patrons from the many illegal all-night rave facilities that thrived in this particular neighborhood. The decor was typical of most alternative Goth clubs: black walls and black flooring, intense white strobes over the dance floor, and use of minimal lighting in the form of torches scattered throughout the periphery of the club. Scarlet velvet was the traditional material of choice, and it flowed thickly across the ceding and gathered into curtains along sections of wall, a blaze of blood-red accent. The bar, which framed one half of the massive dance floor in half-moon fashion, was stunning. Formed of black marble with blood-red vein, it was accented with red jasper and gold, and lines of elegantly formed goblets hung suspended above the well stocked bar.

Above the dance floor, huge banks of video displays hung, facing in all directions. On them flashed scenes of death and destruction; dips from horror movies intermingled with music videos from groups such as The Cure, AC/DC, and Black Sabbath. These dark images flashed and pulsed to the rhythm of one of the finest sound systems in all of Atlanta. Cupping the opposite side of the dance floor, again, in half-moon form, were eight bays of private booths, each containing a half circle bench and a small table for intimate gatherings. Affording privacy if needed, heavy silver chains hung over the bays, allowing those inside the luxury of voyeurism into the world of the club outside, yet allowing enough seclusion for any imagined activity favored by the young. It was into this separate world of reality that I stepped one fateful night, and felt the excitement of a new city, a new club, and new people like me.

I wanted to experience all that this lifestyle had to offer, and to participate in everything this club in particular could give me. I arrived early on my first visit here, wanting to get accustomed to these new surroundings. I purchased a glass of expensive Merlot and positioned myself in a corner booth, allowing me full view of this wonderful haven that lay before me. As the hours passed, the throngs of revelers ebbed and flowed, creating a parade of amazing sights and sounds. The young danced and frolicked to the throb of music while the older patrons, although not truly "old," merely in their 30's, lounged casually in the bar area, observing the wild exuberance of youth in much the same light as I did.

The demeanor and clothes of my fellow revelers were for the most part contrived and created to mirror the creatures we worshiped and desired to be like;

fashioned after the wardrobes worn in the gothic novels that were the guides used to transform our parallel lives. Young men with flowing tresses wore rich velvet waist-coats and tight leather trousers. Many copied the styles of Elizabethan England and the 17th Century French Courts—flounces and feathers, and jackets of brocade and silk. Others wore spiked multi-colored hair, black jeans and high platform boots, with black leather jackets dripping with, chains slung across their shoulders. The women who caught my eye and fueled my fantasies were those attired in exquisite period gowns of satin and lace, their low cut bodices and tightly clinched corsets overflowing their bosoms to fine advantage. It was an eclectic blend of dark fashion and edgy club clothes, and as I watched this pageantry of clothing history pass before me, I dreamed of what could be, and what fantasies I could play out among these fascinating creatures.

As the hour grew late, the crowds grew edgier; trendier, and the music pulsed louder, I was about to leave, finding the continual noise and growing rowdiness among the crowd tiresome, but I vowed to myself a return visit, and soon. Here gathered Atlanta's young and alternative Goth population; people who I hoped would embrace me in time, and I felt at home in the grand and opulent surroundings, I felt I could be accepted here. I felt alive.

As I made my final path across the dance floor and towards the bar and door, amidst the spectacle of the pierced and tattooed, I saw her. She glowed like a candle burning in the darkest of night. Gods! She was breathtaking... captivating... and I was her slave at first sight. Her body was slim, compact, and strong, yet feminine at the same time. She wore black leather pants and a red velvet cowl. The bodice was trimmed in black lace, and its low, off the shoulder style showed me the form of her breasts and the glow of her skin. I savored the smallest detail - the curve of her neck, the line of her jaw, and I stared at her beauty and immediately wanted to know what mysteries were hidden behind her clothes. At that exact moment her eyes found mine, looking as if into my soul. I felt my cheeks burn red with embarrassment, feeling as if my desire for her was suddenly known. I quickly recovered my composure, and with a displayed boldness 1 did not feel, I lifted what was left in my goblet and drained the glass in honor of her beauty. When the glass was empty, and I looked ahead towards her, she was gone.

Feeling the fool, a complete imbecile, I decided to steady my pride with another glass of wine from the bar. Knowing this beauty had just arrived, I hoped to observe tier further, and if my drink did its job as I hoped, I longed to find courage to approach her before the evening ended. I steadily made my way through the mingling masses, and finally reached the bar. After making prerequisite eye contact with those on either side of me, I caught the attention of the bartender and ordered another drink. Full glass finally in hand, I turned and leaned up against the bar as I searched the throngs for this beautiful stranger.

Within moments, I saw her again. Up close she was even more remarkable than she was from a distance. She smiled at me slightly, almost shyly, as she wound her way through the crowd towards me. "Thank you," she said as she casually took the goblet out of my hands. Her voice was light and airy, sparkling in tone; almost girlish, yet at the same time worldly as well. I watched as she brought the goblet to her lips and took only the smallest sip to moist her lips slightly. Her eyes never left mine, and I ordered a second glass for myself. Without a word, we turned and walked towards a vacant booth. She led the way, and I followed, enjoying the gentle sway of her body as she maneuvered through the crowd. Oh, how gracefully she moved! How sensually her hips swayed, and how poised her back remained with each step. And that skin! As flawless as alabaster, I wanted to touch it; to caress her shoulders, her back, her neck, all perfectly shaped. I don't know if any of you have ever felt love at first sight, but for me, this surely was it! My every desire was to touch her—to make love to her. Bodily passions, lust of flesh, and love of beauty...this is what I experienced, and my body responded eagerly to her every movement as she walked ahead of me. My fall from grace? Hardly! But, the threads of my fate were changed forever at this moment.

We made our way to a vacant booth and we sat down. It was then that she told me her name, Gloria; her voice sang it sweetly as if it was a hymn, and she was truly named, for she was a glory to behold. I told her my name In exchange, James, and she repeated it, rolling it on her tongue as if to savor it. I found it entrancing to hear such an ordinary name spoken with such uncommon eloquence. She made my name special, flavoring it with an accent I could not fail to recognize as Irish, I have a weakness for the lilt of an Irish brogue, and her entire look- the red hair, green eyes, and her milky white skin were the final nails for my coffin. I was a dead man.

We talked the better part of what remained of that evening, well past the hour of midnight. As the club started to wind down, and took on that deserted feel, she suddenly stood and said it was time for her to go. I did not want to let this beautiful angel out of my sight, but she assured me that we would see each other again soon, and she leaned in to give me a kiss to seal the promise. I literally swooned at her touch, rocking on my heels and crushing her to me, my hands taking more liberty then I would normally allow. I was ready to have her at that very moment, and I did not want to let her go, but I was not one to force myself, so let my hands fall away. I do not know if it was the forceful passion of my kiss that caused it, but HI tell you this; she had somehow cut her own tongue, filling my mouth with her blood as we kissed. Surprised, I instinctively swallowed it and stood frozen, hypnotized by her beauty as I stared longingly at her.

As if reading the desire in my mind, she changed her mind about leaving and took my hand in hers. She led me willingly along the edge of the seating area to a small opening in the wall. Almost totally obscured by draped velvet, I hadn't noticed the opening earlier. We entered into a small area behind the throbbing walls of the club, not much larger than storage area really, but within a few paces there stood an ornate wrought iron spiral staircase that led upwards about 15 feet to what appeared to be a landing. Gloria continued to lead the way, and again I took full advantage of her magnificent views as I followed her closely up the staircase. Once we reached the top, I could faintly see in the darkness a row of 10 doors that stretched out along the length of the landing. There were no opulent fixtures on this level as no efforts had been made to make this area visible to anyone who might glance up from the floor below. The only color against these dull, black walls was an occasional gold key that hung from a simple hook by several of the doors. Gloria gracefully made her way down to-one of these rooms, gently slid the key off its hook, and unlocked the door. My heart raced with anticipation at what I was about to behold.

She entered before me. The door opened its arms and the room embraced us both in warm darkness. The air was thick with the scent of sweet musk. I could faintly hear the muffled beat of the music from the club below, a hyperactive rhythmic thud, thud, thud. Suddenly, as the door closed behind us, ornate cast iron torches lit up all around the room as if by some invisible force. The flames burned intense then dimmed to- a soft amber glow. My eyes struggled to adjust to the light, and though not blinding, I found I had difficulty focusing. There she was, standing in the far corner of the room. My eyes slowly drifted from Gloria to observe my surroundings.

The first thing I noticed was a large four poster bed in the middle of the room. It was adorned with an impressive dark wood headboard on which were carved the faces of goblins and mythical creatures. The entire bed was covered in the blackest of satin I had ever seen, and the tail posts were draped in red velvet swags that flowed down and spilled onto the floor. On the walls, which were painted in the color of blood, hung velvet ropes and silver chains with handcuffs. Another wall displayed grotesque looking feather masks, leather whips and bindings. Various instruments that could inflict pleasure and pain also hung there. On a small table near the bed a silver chalice had been placed. A collection of knives, long metallic needles and razor blades had- been carefully arranged around it. What was this place?

The music became quieter and the throbbing seemed to come from inside my head now. I felt strangely detached from my body. Gloria took me by the hand and led me over to the bed. She didn't speak; she motioned for me to sit on the edge of the bed. I did not disobey. Her eyes gleamed as she looked at me, flashing red - or was I just imagining it? When she moved she seemed to glide, as if her feet barely touched the ground, as if she was floating. I sat on the bed and felt my body and mind go numb. I tried to speak, but no words came out of my mouth. It was as though my throat was being constricted. Gloria smiled and put her hand over my lips. "Don't say anything now," her voice sounded like sweet pleasure and pain at the same time. Her hand was cold, chillingly so. Her fingers were thin and pale and her fingertips adorned with crimson red nails. The thought of her delicate fingers touching me sent a shiver down my spine. Oh how my body was aching for hers. I lay back and closed my eyes, listening to her move around the room. I slowly opened my eyes again and to my surprise Gloria was now wearing a black, see-through robe, her fiery red hair glistening in the dim light of the torches. Had I fallen asleep? Everything was in a haze and happening in. slow motion.

Gloria handed me the goblet and made me drink some sweet sticky liquid. The taste was that of honey at first, then bitter, and as it hit the back of my throat it burned with an intense heat that spread all through my body, into the very tips of my fingers and toes. It reached my insides, churning and twisting, writhing and stirring; lulling my senses, intoxicating me with this potion she had given me. My senses were a riot; the glow of the torches turned into fierce beams of light, the carved figures on the headboard were pulling grotesque faces; baring their ugliness, cackling, hissing and spitting, baring white fangs. The shadows cast by the flame torches were now dancing on the walls and reflecting against the mirrored ceiling like a ballet of ghosts-twirling, jumping, pirouetting, swaying, and gracefully moving all around. I looked up at the ceiling and saw Gloria facing me. How could this be? She was looking down on me, suspended in the air. The robe she was wearing floating to the ground, she was now naked. I must have been dreaming, for this was not natural. It was not human. She was not human! A slight fear ran through me. My instincts told me to flee, run, and get away. But she was telling me to stay. She shackled me with her thoughts. Her lips not moving as she spoke. She was talking to me using her mind. To anyone walking in on us now, this would have been a very bizarre picture; I restrained by invisible shackles that she had cast upon me, and her floating just below the ceiling, looking down on me.

She slowly descended upon me, her hair flowing, her arms outstretched. She floated till she was sitting on top of me, like a rider on a horse. I looked at Gloria, her face changing from that of my innocent angelic beauty to that of a sultry wicked temptress. Although she did not drink from the goblet, I noticed a tiny drop of something fall from her lips and onto her breast, trickling slowly downwards toward her stomach. Her skin was pearlescent, almost transparent in contrast to the dark spill on her. She looked at me and took my head in her hands and guided me towards it. She made me lick the tiny drop from her perfectly formed breast, guiding me along the dark trail downwards. How sweet it tasted. How intoxicating. My tongue touching her skin was like a lightning bolt racing through my entire body. I licked and sucked on her and she pressed my head harder against her breast. Her chest rising and falling faster, her fingers digging into my skull, urging me not to stop. Even if 1 had wanted to, I could not have let go of her now. Her skin under my tongue, releasing her poisons that would paralyze me - 1 was in ecstasy. She was working her wicked magic. She was the master and I was her slave,

Her sheer beauty left me unable to move. The room was spinning around me. I had lost all sense of time, of self. 1 grabbed her petite waist and gently drew her closer to me. She looked so fragile, an almost child like body, yet she possessed immense strength. Her skin so white, she glowed as she straddled me. She grabbed my left wrist and handcuffed it to the bed. Before I could protest she had cuffed my other wrist and secured me to a large metal hook on the headboard. I was now enslaved to her. But was this not what I had wanted? 1 started to have doubts again. Without using her hands she removed my pants and eased herself back on top of me. She let out a small, eager growl when she noticed my excitement. Her eyes flared up red and 1 was hypnotized, unable to take my gaze away from hers. She lowered herself down to my lips and we kissed for the second time. Her lips were so plump and sweet; like a ripe fruit ready to burst. We kissed with such passion, such wanting and desire. She pressed her body so tight against mine I could feel her heart beating against my chest and feel her breath brush against my skin. Her kisses covered my face and my lips, which she hungrily sucked and bit. The tip of her tongue playfully swirling down and along the pulsating vein on my neck,

With one swift move of her body she had taken me inside of her. Her kisses were electric but this was the force of an entire lightning storm surging through my body to my aching, throbbing loins. I took in a gasp of air, filling my lungs with much needed oxygen, as 1 could easily have forgotten how to breathe at this moment of ecstasy. I had never before experienced anything like this. Until now 1 had never experienced anyone like Gloria. She felt so surreal. We moved together in slow motion unison. She was gently rocking back and forth, her hips moving in a circular motion. She purred and growled contentedly, like a big cat, scratching at my chest and digging in her nails. She was obviously not afraid to show me that she was enjoying herself. Enjoying me inside of her. To say that I was simply enjoying myself as well would have been an understatement. I felt as though we were floating. Our minds merged, we were so close. She scratched me and bit me and the pain was intensely pleasurable. She had almost turned into an animal, a wild animal playing with its prey. She made me suffer. She made me writhe underneath her, frustrated at not being in control; I moaned and tried to manipulate her movements, but she was too strong for me. Her thighs pressed hard against my hips, restricted my every move - had 1 been able to move

Her motions quickened and with every move she took me deeper and deeper inside of her. We were both near rapture, near release from this heavenly, devilish torture. Suddenly she stopped and we gazed into each other's eyes. We were so close in that moment, yet worlds apart. She whispered something in my ear. It was a language I did not understand and one I never heard anyone speak before, but it sounded beautiful coming from her. Then, with one move of her hips I was released from my agony and powerful waves of pleasure washed over me. Gloria let out a big satisfying sigh and her body became rigid for a few seconds. She smiled at me and revealed a big set of shiny white fangs, or so I thought...

What happened next, I cannot remember, I fell into a deep slumber at that moment and awoke sometime during the night to find myself in the alley behind the dub—I have no idea how long I had been there, or how long I slept. How did I get there? I awoke not quite knowing what had just happened to me. Had anything happened at all, or had I been somehow drugged and imagined all this?

Confused and somewhat disoriented, I picked myself up and made my way home in the darkness. Uneasy thoughts accompanied my journey, filling my head with strange images and blurred recollections, none of it making sense. Were these fragments of some dream that haunted me? Surely this could not be real! When I reached my small studio apartment, I suddenly felt exhausted. It was all I could do to kick off my shoes and make my way to the bed. I fell into the waiting comfort of it and fell asleep quickly, but it wasn't restful. Vivid dreams invaded my slumber. Dreams of Gloria. Gloria lying naked in my arms, Gloria swimming in a lake, beckoning me to enter. I dreamed of Gloria lying beside me in the grass, her hair framing her lovely face. A lifetime spent with Gloria passed before me during the night—her touch on my skin, my lips on hers, our bodies joined together.

When the light of morning jolted me awake, sweat covered my body. My heart raced and my head pounded. Dazed, I lay there motionless, trying to make sense out of the events of the previous evening, yet unable to focus my thoughts upon anything but the beauty of my new found love. My body ached, my limbs felt weak, and I struggled to rise from the bed and make my way to the shower.

The hot water poured over my body as I stood in the shower, easing some of the aches but strangely inflicting fiery pricks of pain across my shoulders and chest. I looked down to find the source of this stinging and reeled to see red welts, long scratches and bruises that peppered my torso. Surely these wounds were caused by some forgotten fight from the night before. Surely... My thoughts raced. Was my beloved capable of this? Could this be possible? Were they made in some frenzy of passion, or was there something more?

I hurried off to work, pushing the confusing thoughts that plagued me to the back of my mind. Instead, my thoughts were wonderful daydreams of Gloria. I could not get her out of my mind; she haunted me. Being new in town, I had recently started a job working construction in a local subdivision. My days were spent hammering nails and cutting lumber, mostly solitary work, so my mind was free to wander wherever it chose to go, and as long as my work was completed at day's end, I was left alone. On this day, my unusually withdrawn behavior went unnoticed, and the workday was quickly at an end.

I had decided to go back to the club that night. There were many unanswered questions about the previous night that gnawed at me, and throughout the day I had internal battles with myself over what had happened—what was real, and what was delusion. And, strong amid my internal conflicts and brief recollections of grotesque, nightmarish demons was my deep desire to seek out my Gloria once again. \ longed to see her and be with her. Maybe she had answers for my questions. Maybe she knew the truth of what happened. I had to see her again.

After a hurried shower, I dressed and headed out to the Cavern early. I could have used the MARTA system to reach the club, but I decided to walk; my nervous energy not allowing me to wait any longer to get my mission underway. I grabbed a burger, which I ate on the way. The evening was comfortably warm for a fall night, and in fact, I'd say the weather was perfect, I had plenty of time; the night was early, so I slowed my pace and enjoyed the evening.

The sun was just setting as I neared the club. I paid the doorman, quickly showing my fake ID, as I was not yet 21, and entered. The place was nearly empty this time of day. Besides the bartender, the bouncer, and the four waitresses, I could count the number of other people here on one hand. I engaged in small talk with the staff, and learned that the bartender's name was Frank, and one of the waitresses wore "Marie" on a nametag she had pinned at her waist. I ordered a glass of red wine for myself, and gave Marie a nice first tip of the night. Once again, the parade of people flowed through the main doors. I kept my eyes locked on it, searching for the tell-tale sign of Gloria, that mane of fiery red hair. The first hour passed slowly; the second...third...still no sign of her. It wasn't until after 10:00 pm that she finally came through the door. As rapidly as my heart raced to see her, it sunk, for beside her was a man, perhaps in his mid twenties, his arm draped around her shoulder. His hair was long, black, and sleek, pulled back in a ponytail. I loathed him immediately. I moved to get up, but a quick look and a shake of Gloria's head threw me back into my seat. There were others gathered about the two of them, laughing and joking. I sat there watching them, but wanting only Gloria. They moved through the bar, like a forceful ship that divided the sea of people. They took up residence at a large table, and there they held court, this well-dressed, youthful and vibrant young pack. Marie, the waitress brought a large tray of glasses and a carafe without being asked, which told me they were no strangers to this place. I was the stranger here, the trespasser, not them. Even so, I would not give her up, my Gloria.

Just as I was giving thought to fighting this man, this obvious leader, he turned his face and looked right at me. It seemed that he looked right through me. And he neither smiled nor scowled. He merely gazed at me with no expression at all upon his face. Had he noticed me staring at Gloria? Without turning away, he pulled her to him, and then kissed her hair. The intimacy of it, the familiarity, and the distinct challenge stunned me. And then he smiled at me, but there was no warmth in it, no emotion. In anger I got up and walked straight out the door.
In the cool night air rage and hatred burned through my body, but I was no fool. Including the females, excluding my Gloria, there were eight of them and only one of me. To fight them all, here and now, would only be stupid. As young and strong as I was, I was far from invincible with the odds so high against me. Nor was I suicidal. I would bide my time and hope that my patience paid off.
My evening ruined, and my mood grown sour, I left the club and walked. I didn't care in which direction I went. Anger fueled my steps in the general direction of home, and I walked. I may have wandered for an hour or more, I really can't remember, but when I did take notice of my location I was south of Grant Park. I had walked too far and had to turn around and retrace my steps back. Cutting across the grass to shorten my journey, I heard my name called from within a small cluster of trees.

I spun around to find Gloria standing in the shadows. Her face saddened. She came towards me, and I had a hundred questions on my lips, but she silenced them with her own. Again, her blood filled my mouth, the taste both repulsive and exhilarating; I could feel my mind and body racing, fragments from the night before coming back to me in shards of broken glass. I can't say what happened in those moments when I drank in her life into my very own. All I recall is that we ended that wonderful kiss lying in the grass, me on my back, and her lying on top of me, her body pressing down upon me eagerly.

My hands were caressing the slope of her back, trailing down towards the roundness of her tender curved butt, holding it firmly within my grasp and pulling her tight against me. I kissed her

Again, a human kiss this time, filled with all the passions of my dreams. I ran my fingers through her soft red curls. I kissed her along the neck down to her bare shoulders, nibbling on her exquisitely outstanding collar bone. I raked her flesh with my teeth, leaving red marks on her ivory skin. Suddenly she stopped. Pinning me to the ground with her considerable strength, she stared at me from above.

"Not here," she whispered. "I know a place, just up Cherokee Avenue." I would have followed her to the gates of hell if she led the way. And, just like that we were off...

Those of you who know Atlanta can easily guess where she led me. North we went, hand in hand, stopping along the way only long enough to kiss and fondle each other in lusty anticipation. Before I knew it, we had gone over the short bridge that crossed the beltway and there we stood before the gated entrance of a graveyard. Oh, I thought, what a wonderfully wicked idea!

We entered through a break in the fence and slipped deep into the shadows and among the tombstones in what looked to be the oldest part of the cemetery. The tall granite headstones cast shadows along our path, and we fought through tangles of overgrown brush till we reached a stately gray obelisk that shone white in the moonlight. Here we turned left and Gloria led me along a line of trees and partly toppled markers until we reached a magnificently carved house of the dead. I paused outside for a moment to admire the Roman styled architecture while Gloria easily pushed open the door to the crypt. Once open wide enough to allow us inside, she gracefully slipped in.

By the glow of the candles she lit, I let my eyes soak in the interior. To the left and right, vaults lined the walls four high. In the center of the crypt stood a raised dais of three steps, and in the middle of the platform, a lone marble sarcophagus stood. It was a simple rectangular structure, free of any adornments.

I turned back to find Gloria watching me, her very presence an intoxicant. I went over to her and embraced her, drawing her close to me and kissed her passionately. Trying to free her from the constriction that was her clothes, my fingers worked furiously at the tight laces of her bodice, it finally fell away exposing her firm alabaster breasts with their pale pink nipples, like an open rose sitting atop a whipped cream peak. Immediately my mouth was upon them, licking and sucking at her, her hair entangled in mine. Breathlessly, I quickly worked till her tight leather pants were discarded, exposing the black thong she always wore underneath. Finally, my wish coming true, she stood naked before me. She appeared like a marble statue with flawless skin and perfectly formed body. I wanted to possess her. She was my Celtic Goddess, my Arthurian Morgan la Fey, temptress of my dreams.

My shirt was torn away from me, being cast aside as she undid my pants. She did so with incredible skill and ease, her fingers working fast and precise. As I was freed, she knelt before me and I felt her take me into her mouth, her tongue playing with me before suckling me with a lightning fork tongue, the slow rhythmic motions bringing me to quick breaths and moans. With surprising strength, she pushed me back and lifted me up on top of the sarcophagus, forcing me to lie back as she mounted me; the cold stone chilling me as my body burned for her. I watched her as she lowered herself onto me, her hand gripping me firmly, guiding my throbbing manhood inside her. Once deeply imbedded, she closed her eyes, her teeth lightly biting on her lower lip, as she started to ride me like a wild horse.

My hands were drawn towards her soft inner thighs, the smooth skin yielding under my fingertips. They moved up towards her hips, holding her waist as she rose up and down on me. I moved my hands up past her smooth stomach to find those beautifully shaped breasts, my fingers seeking those rose bud nipples, I gently pinched and roiled them between my fingertips, a cry of pleasure escaped from her as her body went taut, fingernails digging into my bare chest. Pulling her closer towards me, I kissed her deeply, my tongue seeking out hers. Our bodies entwined.

She was suddenly seeking out my neck and chest, licking up the tiny trickles of blood that oozed from crescent shaped wounds made by her long sharp talons. Savoring every drop, she then moved down to where I was still hard, still longing for her. I felt her hot tongue move over me, circling and swirling, cleaning me of her juices. I looked down at her and all I could see was her blaze of hair as she worked her way back up to me, her breasts lightly touching my skin, sending shivers through my entire body.

She took my right hand into hers, slowly lifting it to her mouth, kissing and licking it gently. Then, a piercing pain as her sharp fangs penetrated the skin of my wrist. I knew she had bitten me and she was now drinking my blood. Her naked form above me, my wrist pressed against her mouth, it seemed the most natural of things. She drank from me and I watched her, watched the motion of her throat with each mouthful she swallowed. When she had finished she released my arm, slight puncture wounds still visible, still oozing my blood, my life force. She then raised her own wrist to her teeth, tearing open her white flesh and pressing the bleeding wound to my mouth, urging me to drink. Oh, I drank, drank deep and long. I sucked on her wrist like a newborn at its mother's breast. And, the more I drank, the more I wanted. I could hear my heart pounding in my ears and feel my senses awaken, exploding, my taste buds sang as if they tasted the sweetest of honey for the very first time. The flow of her crimson nectar slowed and then stopped. I let her arm fall gently, the mouth of her wounds slowly closing and then disappearing. She had been watching me the entire time, with those beautiful green eyes. Her steady gaze held no emotion at all.

She smiled at me contented, kissing me, caressing me with her soft lips. I could taste my blood on her. We had shared our blood, we had formed an alliance. She pressed her delicate body hungrily against mine, igniting my passions once more. I took her underneath me, took her with abandonment. I was overcome by a sudden strength, a force I had never felt before. Thrusting myself into her, deep into her temple of womanhood. My battering ram breaching the doors to seek the delicious sanctuary within. I took her with all my strength and skill, my animalistic lust spent on the altar of her body, time and again, until I was weakened, collapsing between her welcoming thighs.

I don't recall when I fell asleep in her arms, or how I came to be resting on the floor, or even when she left me. I awoke upon the cold granite floor, sunlight streaking in the stained-glass windows on the east wall. The candles had long extinguished themselves, leaving a trace of hardened wax along the edge of the floor. I looked around for my clothes, and finding all of them, I hurriedly dressed to the nearing sound of a leaf blower.

Feeling strong and fit for the world, I went outside to greet the day and make my way home. The caretaker, dressed in drab tan work clothes, accosted me as I stepped from the mausoleum. The daylight hurt my eyes and created a dull ache in my head. Shielding my eyes, and having no patience for the man, I left him muttering about damn kids having no respect for the dead, and made my way back to my apartment. I closed the door and drew the curtains tight. Man, what a hangover I had! The darkness was a balm to my seemingly injured eyes. Luckily it was Saturday or I would have lost my job for sure. I went to the small refrigerator, but my stomach rolled as I glanced over its contents. I must be coming down with a touch of the flu, or maybe it was just a really bad hangover. Or, so I thought.

I closed the refrigerator door, opting instead for a shower. I needed it. The warm water felt wonderfully soothing as it cascaded over me. The soap smelted especially strong, but then with the headache, everything was standing out in strong contrast. Rinsing off, I stepped from the shower feeling a little refreshed. I toweled dry and padded barefooted back into the one room studio. I sat down, towel still around my waist and watched the mid day news. A fire on the North side, a drive-by shooting just west of where I lived, a string of city-wide break-ins, and a body found in Grant Park. What?! I turned up the volume.
"Early this morning, while walking her dog, a lady found the body of a homeless man lying in some bushes here at Grant Park. Police haven't released any information at this time. The homeless man is described as being 5' 10" and about 150 pounds. He had shoulder length brown hair, and he was in his late 40's. As soon as more information becomes available..."

I was stunned! Gloria and I had been in that very park! Had the death been from natural causes, or foul play? I shut off the TV and decided I needed some coffee. Yes, some Irish coffee. Heavy on the whiskey... The next night was rather pleasant, the rains having rolled through earlier, washing the air to a sparkling crispness. I opted to take the MARTA subway north from Five Points Station to reach the bar, foregoing my Harley this evening in fear that the night sky might open up and catch me unprotected. Besides, I had waited too late to walk, and a ride on my motorcycle would only dampen my trousers with spray from the tires. Even though the rains had stopped, the streets were still wet.

Rounding the corner, I saw the club already alive with a throng of loud revelers hanging around the front doors, waiting for the club to open. I joined them, showed my fake ID once again, and paying the admission to enter, in only a few weeks I would not need my false identification any longer; I was almost 21. The Cavern was packed to capacity as usual, and a live band was set up on the far side of the dance floor. I quickly checked my reflection in the glass door as I entered the club, I was dressed to impress my beloved, should I see her again this night—tight black jeans, polished black boots, a dark gray pullover, and my favorite long leather duster. My sandy blond hair was lightly gelled and brushed back from my face, and I sported a stylish wrap-style sunglass frame with a vermilion mirrored lens, I carried a knife in a sheath parallel to my belt in the small of my back. I gave myself another approving glance before entering, I was hoping for love, but I was ready for almost anything.

I went straight up to the bar, already crowded with people, and ordered my favorite red wine. The waitress Marie was already doing a brisk business, gliding between the tables and bar as I surveyed the crowd looking for Gloria. So far, no sight of her or any of those who joined her table the previous evening. I was admiring the gathered crush of patrons who pushed in rhythm towards the stage and towards the live band that played there when he came up beside me suddenly. I never saw him approach through the haze of the smoke-filled bar, but suddenly he was there, growling into my ear, "So, you would fight me for her? I would crush you like an ant," his Southern accent distinct and deep.

I spun around to face him, having to look up slightly to meet his gaze. Not some small measure of fear ran through me, but mastering myself, I spoke with confidence, "Crush me if you can, but who knows. You might defeat me in the end, but I'd see you gutted like a fish before I died," It was pure bravado on my part. I'd been in my share of fights, but I'd never cut anyone before. The knife was more to scare than to scar.

He laughed a taunting laugh, "If it wasn't for her, you would now lie rotting; flies laying eggs in your flesh. She stopped me from snapping your neck last night. I may still do just that...but no, that would be too easy."

Then, his face turned hard. It wasn't an angry expression that came over him, but a very matter-of-fact one, "You are simply her new pet; something different to amuse her for a time. She will take what she wants from you and then cast you aside ....

And so John began created a mythos for himself, a sort of hopeful tale that he hoped would mirror his actual circumstances, but Death seemed to be the obvious end of his time. John's thoughts on death were just as ethereal and mystical as those concerning his life. The way the life was lived by the individual, the meaning they invested in it with their actions and deeds, informs the meaning of the individual's death. A life squandered is a meaningless death; a life devoted to a cause and a path leaves a brave and noble corpse to be celebrated in death.

*"What do I think about death? Well I have to say that that comes in many forms and each person's death is as unique as they are when you consider all facts of it. Let's face it, that is not simply the ending of the life and it extends outward, affecting others. The context of their life is just as important as the context of their death, for it gives everything a subtle meaning. An activist gun downed by pro government militia for her works defying a corrupt regime creates a tragic death, but also gives it power and transforms her into a martyr and in time elevation to sainthood. A freedom fighter dies for a just cause and is similar to the terrorists who dies in his own cause, which sees as just. They are the same dead. They are seen differently."*

Estonians believe in the Old Ways concerning the dead as much as John. Graveyards and cemeteries are places not of rotting bones and decaying flesh but a receptacle of wandering spirits of the beloved deceased. These people throw bouquets among the buried dead and they eat in the place of the dead. There are days, the Estonians believe, when the dead return home. These are days for celebration. Food is laid out and a party ensues.

Jamaicans also see death as a time of celebration for nine days, which is meant to ensure the passage of the dead to the next phase of life. In a tent next to the house of the deceased, fish and cakes are left out until the Witching Hour, midnight, so the dead can stop by for a quick meal on their journey to the nether regions. There is a celebration of dancing, singing and drinking of 100-proof rum. The celebration goes on for nine days and nights while the ti bon ange hovers over the dead corpse; 40 days later another session of singing takes place when the spirit of the dead stops roaming the earth. Johnnycakes are laid with the corpse for this journey. The gros bon ange then is free to move on to the cosmic community of the ancestors. At the end of these nine days, the houngan, or voodoo priest, then can place the ti bon ange in a jar and burn the jar, releasing the spirit from this plane. Sometimes the spirit is kept trapped in that jar and worshiped in that state. Sometimes the jar is broken and dropped at a crossroads to free the soul.

The Christians of Ireland who lace their Christianity with the Old Ways of the Pagan keep their dead in a wake house and sprinkle salt on the death bed, which was believed to keep away bad spirits. Candles are placed around the bed and lit. Prayers are said for the dead as the mourners walk in and out. Those who knew the dead told stories and recalled the life of the dead person. They all share a pipe full of tobacco. When the mourning is over, the dead man is taken to the burial ground by a long route to fool the Other Ones, the fairies and the others who have died before. Anyone who met with the procession along the way joined in and said prayers for the dead. Then come the "keeners," a tradition that goes back to old Celtic times, who sing and wail laments about the virtues of the deceased. Then the men go to the pub and the women go home.

According to him, in order for John's spirit to be released into the next dimension, the next phase of existence, Summerland, whatever it should be called, John would need four people, one carrying a rock to symbolize the earth, facing North; one carrying a feather to represent the air, facing East; one holding incense and facing South; the fourth person would hold a cup of water facing West. In the center of this circle is an altar that would bear a photo of John. The powers of the elements would be called upon and then the congregants would chant:
"Take me now; take me now
for to face the Other Side.

By the earth and wind and the fire and rain
I'm on my way, remember me.
Then they would all turn to the North and say:
Take me now back to the earth
from which we spring and then return.
I shall cross over, now it is my turn.
I am not afraid Remember me.
All four would repeat this verse as they turned to each of the four directions.
Blood of my blood
Bone of my bone
Flesh of my flesh
Keep my soul alive
I will live on
Within your hearts
I am not afraid
Remember me"

John's ashes would be scattered into the wind and blown throughout Nature. Everyone in attendance would share the good memories of John as his mortal remains fluttered in the air. John's Soul would be free to go not to Heaven to sit at the Right hand of God or to hell to be tormented in a pit of fire; rather, he would go to a place where he would look into a vast, shimmering, cosmic field – a mirror – where he would see what he has done, what was done to him and what he could have done. When his Soul, freed of the flesh, was made better and was ready would be reborn into another carnal vessel for another attempt at this life, having learned the hard lessons of the past.

It was, perhaps, in one of his poems, which reads more like a Romantic piece from hundreds of years ago than something scribbled on spare scraps of paper in today's modern Death Row, that John captures the essence of the thoughts of his impending death and his hopes for resurrection:

"Upon a sea o' glass cast was I -
dark an' calm this abyss didst lie.
Lingering upon its gentle currents borne -
'til thoughts of past remained no more.
Future sights given up as lost -
a sea once calm did churn an' toss.
Into blackness was I thrown-
down deep I sank from surface torn.
Drum beat slow an' even, still -
brightness flash, thunder peal.

In rush breath, a wailing cry -
reborn on earth, to live an' die."

Glossary/Notes

1.  Many caul bearers claim to possess clairvoyance or other preternatural abilities. In Old Europe, the appearance of a caul on a baby was a sign of good luck. It was an omen of greatness and good fortune. Sailors collected cauls because they thought that a baby's caul would protect them from death by drowning. Medieval women made good money off of superstitious sailors. Caul babies were also associated with strong protective magic and the ability to protect the harvest.

2.  The hex that is put on people by Magick was borrowed from the German Hexe, "witch", and related to this is the evil and ugly female "hag". Both trace their origin back to the German word Hexe which seems akin to hedge, another item growing in the country. Thus, a hedge witch was simply one practicing The Craft out in the country among the "pagans" of the countryside. Yet it took on all kinds of negative connotations and stereotypes

3.  A quaich is traditionally a shallow two-handled drinking cup or bowl whose heritage goes back to Scotland. The origins are unclear but most people believe they stem from the Scottish Gaelic word cuach, which means "cup", according to the Encyclopedia Britannica. It was inspired by the low silver bowls with two flat handles used as bleeding vessels (blood calls to blood) the Old World of the 17th century. Some have glass bottoms so that the drinker could keep watch on his companions. The quaich also has a touch of the love spell magic to it: some had a double glass bottom in which was kept a lock of hair so that the owner could drink from his quaich to his lady love.

4.  Tisiphone was one of the Furies, and sister of Alecto and Megaera. She was the one who punished crimes of murder. Alecto is the one of "implacable or unceasing anger" Megaera is the cause of jealousy and envy, and punishes people who commit crimes, especially marital infidelity. Her function is very similar to Nemesis, with the difference that the latter's function is to castigate crimes against the gods. All three were the daughters of Gaea fertilized by the blood spilled from Uranus when Cronus castrated him.

5.  Ogham is an Early Medieval alphabet used primarily to write the Old Irish language Ogham is sometimes referred to as the "Celtic Tree Alphabet." Coll, for instance, meant "hazel tree" or "fair wood" and was linked with the Welsh Collen and eventually our Modern Colleen, the

name and general term for a "fair" young lady. Runes were a proto-Germanic alphabet, the mastery of which was supposed to yield magic.

6. In English folklore, Herne the Hunter is a ghost that haunts Windsor Forest and Great Park in the English county of Berkshire. He rides a dashing steed as he patrols the woods of his domain and, fittingly, had antlers on his head.

7. Lughnassa, also known as Lammas Day, celebrates the first harvest of grain. When the Pagan celebrations were co-opted by the Christian churches, it was traditional to bring a loaf on this day to church that was made from the grain of that first harvest. Could this a precursor to the tradition of a bread wafer representing the Body of Christ? Semantically, in Old English especially, Lugh-nassadh, pronounced phonetically as the language was at the time, has the sound of another Christian name for the holiday, "loaf-mass." This holiday is also known as Gule of August. Few can figure out why. If the "g" in gule is pronounced as it would have been in Old English, the word then sounds like our Modern "Yule," which marks the Christian Christmas (Christ Mass) season. This co-optation was a point of "ire" for John.

8. Wicca is a Neopagan religion. Its adherents are referred to as Wiccans; they are also called Witches or Crafters. Wicca was popularized in the 1950s and early 1960s by a Wiccan High Priest named Gerald Gardner.

9. Cernunnos is another Celtic deity that is associated with nature, stags and is portrayed, like Herne the Hunter, with antlers on his head. The Latin cognate "cornu" means "horn. An important Irish god figure who was characterized as a father figure. His symbols were a bottomless cauldron from no man left unsatisfied and a mighty club with he could slay and restore life. Some believe Danu was his mother. Danu is associated with the land and river, like her namesake the Danu-be River.

10. Llud was a prototypical hero who confronted and defeated dragons and giants to defend his people.

11. Druantia is associated with the fir tree, which is also the root of her name ("drus"). This same root is the root for the word "druid"; thus, she is "Queen of the Druids".

12. (http://www.ourladyswarriors.org/dissent/defpagan.htm)